THE EX-HUSBAND

AN ADDICTIVE AND GRIPPING
PSYCHOLOGICAL THRILLER

AARON QUINN

She got away once. He won't let her escape again.

Published by aaronquinnbooks.com

Copyright @ Aaron Quinn 2024

All rights reserved.

Aaron Quinn has asserted his right to be identified as the author of this work.

No part of this book may be reproduced, stored in any retrieval system, or transmitted in any form or by any means, electronic, mechanical, photocopying, recording or otherwise, without the prior written permission of the author.

This book is a work of fiction, names, characters, businesses, organisations, places and events other than those clearly in the public domain, are either the product of the author's imagination or used fictitiously. Any resemblance to actual persons, living or dead, events or locales is entirely coincidental.

GET YOUR FREE EBOOK

Subscribe to my newsletter and receive your FREE ebook of *The Unwelcome Guest* that's only available to my VIP reader group:

aaronquinnbooks.com

1

THE ALARM JOLTS me from my sleep. It drags me from fading dreams as I reach over for my iPhone to stop the shrill tone that feels like it's drilling into my brain. Even the "Morning Jane" alarm message on the phone screen seems to mock me. I'm not a morning person!

As summer drifts into autumn, the weather always seems to turn in a blink of an eye. With today's cooler temperature, the thought of tearing myself away from under the warm duvet sends an anticipatory shiver through me. I rub my eyes and sigh while gazing at the ceiling, wondering how the nights fly by and yet the days drag on. I push back the duvet and slide out of bed. The cold laminate floor sends a shiver up my legs as I pad to the bathroom. After turning the shower dial up, I wait a few seconds before stepping under the hot spray, letting it wash away the last cobwebs of my disturbed sleep. Steam fills my bathroom and leaves a damp mist which hangs in the air. The bad dreams still chase me in the depths of the night when I least expect them, and I wonder if I'll ever be free of them.

Shampoo slides through my hair, but Mark floods my thoughts. A week has stretched between us, and it feels more like forever. Work, his ever-present shadow, has claimed him again. I ache for the mornings lost, his warmth tangled with mine. Yet, amid the longing, gratitude whispers—at least I have him in whatever fragments time allows. If only...

Halting my thoughts, I rinse away suds, dry off, and wrap myself in my warm dressing gown before I choose an outfit for the day. I rummage through my wardrobe, selecting a modest grey trouser and black top combo. I've always chosen to dress conservatively, avoiding unnecessary attention. Fashion serves as a painful reminder of my past, when all I wanted to do was make myself invisible. I pull my damp hair into a tight ponytail. Time isn't on my side today, so I don't have the time to dry it.

Dressed and looking like a plain Jane, I glance in the wardrobe mirror. The woman staring back at me now is so different from the one who arrived here broken and bruised. At least her eyes are no longer gaunt and lifeless. I survived. I rebuilt my life, one day at a time. And I will never again allow someone to take my power. The past can't touch me now.

With a deep breath, I shoulder my handbag and head downstairs. The old floorboards creak under my feet. When I bought my house, it was still trapped in the seventies and needed to be renovated from top to bottom. The floorboards were the only thing I managed to salvage and restore.

Tea in hand, I look out of the lounge window at the street beyond. My neighbours are getting on with life too, dragging recycling bins to the kerb ready for the dustmen and ushering children into cars ahead of the school run.

The Ex-Husband

An ordinary scene playing out with ordinary lives. Mine is ordinary too now, and though many would disagree or hate it, I am grateful for it. A stable job, a cosy two-bedroom home that I've lovingly given a new lease of life to, and a loving partner—the simple pleasures that once seemed out of reach are now real.

I smile and take a sip of tea before looking at the screen on my phone. "Shit." I notice the time. I'm going to be late.

Before rushing out to the car, I quickly return to the kitchen and leave my mug in the sink, then grab my keys and carefully back out of my small gravel driveway. The morning commute has already begun, a stream of vehicles heading into the city centre which slows me down more than I'd like, but hey, at least the traffic is moving, well... crawling, actually. As I stop and wait at a red light, I glance at the pedestrians walking along the pavement. A mother pushes a pram while on her phone, students walk with heavy backpacks, early morning commuters clutch their coffees like lifelines, a pair of teenagers jostle each other as they laugh at something amusing on their phones, and an elderly man shuffles along as he walks his little dog. I can't help but smile at the pair, with him looking down and his dog looking up at him, almost smiling. *Can a dog smile? I assume so.*

The light turns green, and I continue on my way, merging into more slow-moving traffic. The familiar streets and buildings pass by outside my window as I think about my old life versus where I am now. As I've grown, I've come so far and changed so much. Finally, I am safe, stable, and free.

Taking a quick glance at the passenger seat, my thoughts turned to Mark. I miss his playful banter when he's in the car with me. He always knows how to make me smile, even on the hardest days.

The traffic slows to a snail's pace as I approach the office. I have another busy day at my desk filled with busy work—answering calls, typing reports, and assisting my boss. My job as team secretary to the sales director at a local electrical components firm may not be glamorous, but it provides stability and routine—something I crave after years of chaos and uncertainty. It can be hectic, but I like the pace and the sense of accomplishment. And I've made some friends here too, like Georgia, Clive, and Annette. We have fun together even when the job gets boring.

As I turn into the office car park, I stop at my usual spot, the one I've used every day since I first started. Guess I'm a creature of habit. Gathering my things, I head inside. The sales floor is quiet, with a few of my co-workers tapping away at their computers.

"Morning, Clive!" I call to the tall bald man hunched over the copier. He turns and gives me a friendly smile.

"Alright, Jane! How's you? Kettle's hot if you want a cup."

"Cheers, I've already had one and I'm good, thanks mate. Another day, another dollar," I reply as I drop my bag beside my chair and settle at my desk, switch on my computer, and begin sorting through emails. Most are reminders about upcoming projects and deadlines. I make notes on my planner, carefully lining up the day's tasks.

The elevators ding. Annette and Abnash chat loudly as they walk in together.

"Morning, Janie," Annette chortles in a high-pitched, song-like tone. "How was your evening?"

"Oh. Fine. Just a quiet one at home."

The Ex-Husband

"We should grab a bite to eat again soon, yeah?" Annette suggests.

"Sounds good to me." I appreciate her offer. It's nice to have friends who care. My evenings are often lonely, but I try to focus on the positive.

Abnash doesn't say much. He's not a morning person. And I'm more likely to get a less than polite reply from him if I say too much to him for the first hour until he's had enough coffee or Red Bull.

An hour passes in a blur of emails, phone calls, and office chatter. The sales team filters in, filling the room with life and banter ahead of the morning team meeting that's about to start. I tidy my desk and gather a notepad and pen, then make my way to the conference room.

Brad Ritchie, our director, is already at the head of the table flipping through a stack of papers. He looks up when I enter ahead of the rabble that barge in after me.

"Morning, Jane." Brad looks up and slides a stack of paperwork and invoices towards the space next to him. That's his way of telling me I need to sort this out. He's a man of few words.

Brad clears his throat. "Let's crack on team. We've got a busy day ahead. Let's close the week strong. The Red Sprout order is still pending, so I need all hands on deck to get their revised quote over to them. And don't forget we've also got the Weston bid due by the end of the day......"

As Brad drones on about accounts and deadlines, my mind drifts. I think about Mark, wondering when I'll see him again. But I need to text him this morning to see if he's around this weekend. We usually spend most weekends together, so if he's free tomorrow and not going to football, then it's a few hours until I see him at my doorstep. The mere thought draws a smile across my face as I anticipate the moment he walks through the door and what will hopefully happen right after.

A gentle nudge from Clive pulls me back. I smile as my face flushes. I shift in my seat, hoping no one else clocked me drifting off with my thoughts. For now, work comes first. The rest will have to wait.

2

I BREATHE a sigh of relief when I realise that we've already hit the end of the day. We always finish at four on a Friday so that we can start our weekends early. There are a few of the team who live further out towards Suffolk and Essex, so they appreciate the chance to get ahead of the Friday night rush hour traffic. I want to get off and go home to crash in front of the TV with a pizza and beer, but my workmates, Georgia, Lucy, and Priya, have other plans for me and drag me to a bar in town. Rather than being a party pooper, I think a social beer or two won't harm me, and I can make my excuses as soon as I'm done.

I leave my car at work and together with the girls, walk the short distance to the part of town where most of the work crowd hang out after work. The mood is upbeat as Georgia and Lucy race ahead to get the drinks in. Priya and I aren't in so much of a hurry as we stop every so often in shop windows to see if anything catches our eye.

As we finally arrive and catch up with the others, the bar is packed and noisy, filled with other workers who have the same idea as us. I slide into a booth beside Georgia, her blonde hair tickling my arm as she leans in to give me a quick hug. Georgia is my closest friend at work and someone who I hang out with most lunchtimes. We're polar opposites, but it seems to work. She's loud, flirtatious, cheeky, and a bit of an extrovert, especially with a Prosecco or two inside her.

"Jane! Finally, the bloody weekend is here. I need this beer big time." Georgia waves her bottle and takes a hefty glug that seems to go on for a while.

Lucy and Priya scoot in across from us, giggling about their latest office gossip as they look around to gawk at any good-looking men who might be here. I half-listen, sipping my bottle of Sol, enjoying the light citrus tang.

Georgia nudges me, her green eyes dancing. "So, how's Mark? Have you thought more about him moving in yet?"

My cheeks flush. "It's too soon for that. But things are going well. I'm seeing him tomorrow. He sent me a text this afternoon saying he's free all weekend, which is good."

"Oi oi, that's Jane not getting out of bed this weekend." Priya's eyes widen having eavesdropped on our conversation. "He's such a nice bloke. You've bagged a good one there."

"And fit," Lucy adds with a wink, teasing me as she pushes the neck of her beer bottle in and out of her mouth.

I can't help but smile thinking of Mark. The girls are much more forward than me. I'm more reserved and often find it hard to express myself. Shadows of the past linger; my ex had a way of making my feelings seem like burdens, remnants of his voice still echoing that vulnerability was a flaw. The sign of a weak mind. The conversation flows, work stress melting away. More beers and nachos arrive for our table, and I pick at a few hoping they soak up the booze. I cherish these simple moments with my friends, reminding myself to be present. For now, I push aside lingering anxieties and enjoy the laughter and comfort of friendship.

"Are you doing much tomorrow?" I ask Georgia.

She wipes her wet lips and leans into me so I can hear her above the music now blaring around us. "Girly day tomorrow. Mani and pedi, then getting my lashes done." She flutters her eyelids and then studies my features. "Why don't you come with? You'd look gorgeous with a set of lashes. You can tickle Mark's face with them." Georgia squeals with laughter and I rock back and look shocked at the suggestion.

"Maybe one day. I'm not brave enough yet."

"Come on, Jane." My friend nudges me in the ribs playfully. "Be a devil. Even the girls in high school are getting them done now. It's all about looks these days."

I sigh and smile at Georgia. Everything she tells me goes against everything I've learnt to do to *avoid* attention. How can I tell her the real reason I don't want new nails or lashes? That in the past I was called a slut and whore if I applied a little mascara or lippy. That my husband physically treated me like a common prostitute as a punishment if I tried to look pretty or feminine. There are things I can't tell her though every bone in my body wants her to know. I need her to understand the pain, sadness, and fear I carry with me every day like a heavy clock draped around my neck. It's taken a lot of courage to let Mark take me to bed. At first, it was hard. I would lie there rigid as a board, and Mark would think I didn't like him. But as time went on, I fought hard against the demons within and opened up to him with my mind and body. And now, our physical connection is the one thread I hold on to that makes me feel human and alive.

I nurse my second bottle slowly, not wanting to get drunk. Ever since my marriage, I feel uneasy in public places, hyperaware of people around me. A constant prickle of unease runs through me as if I'm not in full control of my faculties. Being drunk feels like a luxury I can't afford to experience. The bar's crowded tonight and I scan the room, cataloguing the faces. Most seem harmless enough, but you never know.

My friends chat and laugh, amused by some dating app mishap Lucy's regaling us with. In my late teens and early twenties that carefree attitude used to be mine, before my marriage shattered my sense of safety. Now I'm always watchful, suspicious of strangers looking at me or getting too close. I wish I could relax and let loose like them, but my mind won't allow it.

The girls want another round, but I cry off. "I should head home and get the place tidy before Mark comes tomorrow." I give them each a tight hug. "See you Monday."

Outside, the cool night air helps clear my pleasant buzz. Revellers are spilling out of bars around me, their laughter and loud conversations bouncing off the build-ings. There's a good mood in the air as I set off towards home sticking to well-lit streets. The fifteen-minute walk will do me good; help calm my restless thoughts. Besides, I've skipped a few gym sessions recently, so the exercise won't make me feel so bad. I quicken my stride, suddenly craving the comfort of home. Night-time walks used to be my favourite, but now the shadows appear menacing. I hate the fear that courses through my veins, angry he still has this power over me.

I pass a familiar spot where there's always a large crowd lingering. Thankfully, I don't need to be wary of this group since they're waiting for the soup kitchen van.

The Ex-Husband

As I near it on the opposite side, I pause, watching the volunteers hand out steaming cups of soup and sandwiches to the many homeless that call the streets their home. I think it's such a kind thing to help those in need. An idea occurs to me—maybe I could volunteer here someday when I feel stronger in myself. Give back somehow. I've been so focused on my own problems for so long, it would do me good to think of others for a change. I make a mental note to look into it later when I'm feeling braver. Baby steps.

Lost in thought, I startle when a man catches my eye standing behind the table handing out sandwiches. My heart leaps as I recognise him. It's David, my ex. The one I got away from. Before I can react, he vanishes around the back of the van.

I stand frozen, pulse racing as my blood runs cold. My hands are clammy, my legs feel like jelly, and my mouth runs dry. Was it really him or my imagination? Do I confront him or run? Fight or flight kicks in and I rush away. My mind spins—was seeing David real or another trick of my weary mind? I don't know what's real any more. All I can do is get somewhere safe and try to make sense of it all. The familiar panic rises as I hurry away, glancing behind me. *Please, God, no.*

I burst through my front door and quickly lock it behind me, leaning back against it while I try to catch my breath. My heart is pounding as I sink to the floor and draw my knees to my chest. I shut my eyes, replaying the moment I saw him over and over.

Was it really David? But it was dark. The dark can play tricks on our minds. It looked so much like him. That unruly dark hair, those narrow eyes. The crooked smile that used to make me melt when I first met him. But it was only a split second before he disappeared from view. I didn't even get a clear look at his face. Surely it couldn't have been him. Why would he be here, giving out food in Cambridge when he lives in Norfolk? It makes little sense.

I take a few deep breaths and try to calm my racing thoughts. It must have been my imagination playing tricks on me again. Since everything that happened with David, I see danger around every corner. Even a passing resemblance is enough to send me into a tailspin. I've become so paranoid and mistrustful now. I don't feel safe anywhere, even though I try so hard to hide it from everyone, including Mark.

With a sigh, I haul myself to my feet. I need to stop letting my fears control me like this. What I thought I saw tonight wasn't real. David is far away; he can't hurt me now and he doesn't know where I am. At least that's what I keep telling myself.

3

I QUICKLY THROW on my comfy joggers and hoodie, tying my hair up in a high ponytail. Though I look scruffy, I prefer to wear casual and baggy clothes on weekends when I don't have to see anyone apart from Mark. And Mark doesn't mind. Even if I wore a black bin liner, he would still be happy. I hear the door open and hurry from my bedroom, eager to see Mark at the door with a big cheesy grin holding Starbucks coffees and warm croissants from my favourite bakery. I'm thrilled at the treats and his visit after a week apart. His work as an electrician has kept him so busy this past week we've hardly talked.

"Hey, you. Surprise." A cheeky grin splits his face.

He holds out the coffees and pastry bag like an offering. I take them, the smell making my mouth water. "You're the best boyfriend. I've missed you this week."

"Me too." He steps inside and kisses my forehead before staring me in the eyes, his gaze lingering before winking. "Thought we could catch up over breakfast."

I lead him to the kitchen and grab two plates and a few napkins from the kitchen counter before serving up the croissants. We sit across from each other, sip our coffees, and I welcome the warmth it brings. The croissant melts in my mouth, all buttery and flaky.

"How's work been?" I ask, wiping the crumbs from my lips.

He launches into a story about the office building rewire job he's been on, complaining about the fussy manager who hovers over the crew. I'm content to listen, soaking up his soft but manly voice. His face is so animated that I could watch him for hours. I forget my ever-churning thoughts and exist here with Mark, our knees touching under the table.

He gives me a sly smile, raising an eyebrow. "I missed more than your voice this week."

My cheeks flush, but I smile back. "Oh, really?"

He stands up, pulling me up too. "Oh, yeah, I certainly have. How about we continue breakfast upstairs?" he suggests, narrowing his eyes. His powerful arms wrap around my waist as he presses his lips to mine. I melt into his embrace, electricity coursing through me as my body tingles. For a moment, nothing else seems to matter. There are no anxious thoughts, no twisting insides, and no sweaty palms. Mark's the distraction I need right now. I smile back and nod as I take his hand and lead him upstairs to the bedroom, leaving the unfinished breakfast behind.

My heart races as he kisses my neck and whispers how much he wants me. A familiar resistance rises within, but I push it down. I focus on Mark and being present in this moment with him. His hands explore my body with urgency. I let myself get lost in his touch and the intimacy we share, pushing away my doubts and fears. Opting for intimacy instead of withdrawal and the sense of being desired and treasured.

The Ex-Husband 15

Afterwards, we lie tangled in each other's arms, skin against skin. I rest my head on Mark's chest, listening to the steady beat of his heart. His rough fingers trail up and down my back. It feels so good to have him here. I feel safe when he's around me. It's like he could stop a raging herd of bulls from getting past my front door. I want to stay in this cocoon of contentment, but my mind races again. Why won't it give me a break and stop? Doubts and anxieties creep back in. I think of the emotional distance I've kept from Mark, from everyone. How I hold back parts of myself out of fear of getting hurt and being vulnerable. Mark knows me well, but as my boyfriend, not as well as he should. I can't help the constant tidal wave of ruminations. It's like there's a part of my identity trapped in a box deep within my mind and I can't find the key to open it. It's not fair to him or me either. Shifting within the comfort of his embrace, I sigh.

Mark looks at me. "What's on your mind, lover?"

I shrug. "Not much. Just thinking about... us. How sometimes it's hard for me to be present. To open up."

He rolls on his side to face me, brushing a strand of hair from my face with a smile. "I know. But I'm here for you, always. We'll go at your pace. I'm not here to pressure you."

His sincerity and patience overwhelm me. Tears well up. He wipes them away, then pulls me close. "It's alright. I've got you."

I cling to him, letting the tears fall. The high walls around my heart crack open, if only a sliver. I feel naked yet cared for in his arms. Still scared, but a little less alone.

After some time, he kisses my forehead and suggests a shower. I nod, feeling lighter. We head to the bathroom hand in hand, leaving lingering touches and stolen kisses in our wake.

We emerge showered, clothes sticking to still-damp skin. My hair hangs in limp strands, but Mark looks at me like I'm the most beautiful woman alive. He comes over to me and cradles my face in his hands before planting a soft kiss on my lips.

My phone on the bedside table buzzes with a text. I glance down and check the screen. Chrissy again, probably wanting to know if I'm free for coffee. I silence it. Right now, I want to be here with Mark. No disruptions. We head back down and to the kitchen, where I pop the remaining croissants in the microwave while Mark pours the lukewarm coffees into mugs. Steam rises as I remove the buttery pastries. We settle at the small table by the window in the lounge overlooking the street.

Mark flashes me a crooked grin. "Nothing like a cold Starbucks to start the day."

I laugh. "Beats my usual toast on the run."

We chat about nothing as we eat. The world feels small, quiet, and intimate here. No expectations, only an easy connection. I wish we could stay in this bubble a little longer. Mark might get bored, but I'd love it. Too soon, we're rinsing our dishes and heading out hand in hand.

I glance at my neighbour Chrissy's house as we pass, hoping to avoid her this morning. They're lovely really, but... Chrissy and her husband, Alby, are both in their late sixties. Alby is a grumpy man who would much rather do his gardening or hide in his greenhouse than come inside and listen to his wife's non-stop chatter. Chrissy wants to know everyone's business but is harmless really. Chrissy will always find a reason to be in her front garden so she can keep an eye on the comings and goings of everyone in the street.

But it looks like it's not my lucky day as she's already

The Ex-Husband 17

out pruning roses in a hideous floral housedress. "Morning loves!" she calls out. "Prised yourselves apart, eh?" She cackles at her own joke.

I squeeze Mark's hand, bracing myself. Here we go.

Chrissy waddles over towards the pavement, shears in hand. "And where are you two lovebirds off to today, then?"

Before I can answer, Alby appears from behind a hedge towards the side of their house, clippings piled in his wheelbarrow. "Bin men were supposed to come yesterday," he grumbles. "Lazy buggers still haven't shown up."

Chrissy ignores him, her beady eyes fixed on me.

"We're heading into town to do some shopping." Chrissy's nosiness grates on me. She thrives on any morsel of gossip.

"Oooh, how nice!" my neighbour coos. "Say, did you see the fancy car parked at No.27 last night? That Meera's got herself a new fella, I reckon."

I shrug, but Chrissy pushes on without waiting for an answer.

"Big flashy Mercedes. This bloke didn't leave 'til the early hours, can you imagine?" She leans in. "Looked like a proper city type. Slick suit, briefcase. Bet he's married too, the cad."

I resist the urge to say anything. Chrissy's imagination runs wild with half-truths and assumptions.

Mark squeezes my hand, sensing my irritation. "Well, we should be off. I have an urgent appointment later today. Have a nice day, you two."

Chrissy looks disappointed she couldn't dredge more gossip out of me. But she recovers quickly. "Ta-ta! Enjoy your shopping!"

As we walk away, I breathe a sigh of relief. The further

from Chrissy's prying eyes, the better. "Urgent appointment? That's news to me."

Mark nudges my shoulder. "I don't, but it's the first thing that popped into my head." He laughs as we scurry away.

Mark and I stroll hand in hand down the pavement towards his van, leaving my neighbour and her grouchy husband behind. The brisk spring air feels refreshing after being cooped up all week. Mark looks relaxed and happy, his warm brown eyes crinkling at the corners as he smiles down at me.

"Glad to get away from the neighbourhood patrol?" he teases as he squeezes my hand.

I laugh. "Chrissy means well, but she doesn't know when to quit."

Having driven the short distance and parked up, we cross the street and join the crowds heading towards the city centre. The Grand Arcade looms ahead, its gleaming floors and sky lit ceilings beckoning. Mark holds the door for me as we step into the din of shoppers.

My eyes roam over the displays. "Ooh, let's pop into Zara." I make a beeline for the entrance and feel the waft of warm air bathe my face from the heating ducts above the doorway.

Mark indulges me good-naturedly as I sift through racks of dresses. I hold up a blue fit-and-flare against myself. "What do you think?"

"Gorgeous. Though not as gorgeous as you." He punctuates this with a peck on my cheek.

I flush, swatting his arm playfully. "Liar." But his compliments always make me smile.

We meander along, peeking into shoe stores and more clothes shops. There's nothing we need in particular, but it's great having a mooch around the shops. The hours slip by. With Mark, even mundane things feel fun. No one else can make me laugh so easily or feel so cared for and he's always within touching distance. I love being with him.

We wander outside, the smells of nearby restaurants making our stomachs rumble. I check my watch. "Blimey, it's nearly two p.m. Shall we pop into The Driftwood for a bite?"

Mark agrees. He's always hungry. We stroll down the cobbled side streets to the pub. He holds open the heavy wooden door as we step inside. The interior is all dark wood and low lighting, with a fire crackling in the hearth. We settle into a corner booth and a chipper waitress takes our order of fish and chips twice, and before long our food arrives piping hot, the batter perfectly crispy and the chips chunky and fluffy inside. Between bites, we chat about nothing in particular—work gossip, home repairs, and weekend plans. I've been wanting to change all my ceiling lights upstairs, so it's handy that Mark is a sparky. He offers to do it for me if I choose the fixtures.

Sitting with Mark, passing a lazy afternoon, I feel so chilled and, well... normal. At this moment, I have everything I need. But we stop in mid flow when a couple at a table towards the other end of the pub raise their voices. I crane my neck to see what the commotion is about, as does Mark. It's a couple arguing. My stomach lurches as I see the man lean into his partner and hiss something that has her pulling away. Everyone is watching now as the man continues to shout at her, slapping his hand on the table. I feel my heartbeat quicken as I watch her reaction. She's close to tears. I find it hard to breathe, and... So much of me wants to run over and jab my fork into the man's eyes. He's humiliating his partner in public, something I can relate to first-hand, so I know how she's feeling.

Bar staff rush over to calm the situation, but the man doesn't listen. His partner pushes back her chair and rushes for the door in floods of tears with him in hot pursuit as they both disappear outside.

The silence around the pub is soon replaced by hushed conversations. I glance across to Mark who shrugs his shoulders. Suddenly, I've lost my appetite.

4

My SHOULDERS ACHE as I slump against my seat and stare out of the van window. The streets of Cambridge bustle with students milling between shops, and tourists meander along pavements, gazing into windows of quaint stores which look as if they've been here since the start of time. A relaxed vibe settles over the city. It's why I moved here—such an eclectic mix of people that I could watch for hours.

Mark steers the van through the narrow streets as I scan the crowds. Then a fleeting glance of a familiar face catches my eye. He emerges from a shop, but before I can blink again, disappears into the throng.

I gasp. Twice now. My mind spins as it grapples to process what I've seen.

"What's wrong?" Mark asks.

Is it really him? Or are my eyes playing tricks, like the other night when I had one too many beers? Now stone-cold sober, I wrestle with making sense of what I glimpsed.

It can't be David. Please, God, no!

My knuckles whiten as I clench the door handle. The pit of nausea in my stomach churns at the mere thought of him sliding back into my life. After all these years, he can't be here. Cambridge is my haven, my escape from the ghosts of my past and a place I could start afresh. I swallow hard, steadying my ragged breaths. "Nothing. I thought I saw someone I knew."

Mark frowns but keeps his eyes on the road. "An old friend?"

If only Mark knew the real horrors of my ex-marriage. He knows David was a bastard to me, and how with the help of my best friend, Anita, I escaped my abusive marriage. I spared him the graphic detail, but he filled in the gaps himself. I force a weak smile. "No, I don't think so."

Silence fills the space between us, Mark's unspoken concern hanging in the air. But he knows better than to pry. My past remains locked away where it belongs.

The streets blur as we drive on through the city. But a single question echoes in my mind and refuses to fade into the background.

Back home, Mark heads straight for the sofa and grabs the remote to flick through the sports channels. The familiar drone of match commentary soon fills the room. I busy myself in the kitchen, opening and closing cupboards. My hands tremble as I fill the kettle, spilling water across the counter. I curse under my breath, mopping it up with a tea towel.

Focus, Jane.

But my thoughts keep spiralling back to those familiar icy blue eyes. David's eyes. The way they would darken before his temper erupted. No. I dig my nails into my palms, steadying myself against the sink as I stare through the window towards my small grassy garden. *You're being ridiculous*. Cambridge is miles from Norfolk, from our old life. I'm safe here. Happy.

The kettle boils, steam hissing as I pour water into two mugs. As I dunk the tea bags, I glance through the doorway at Mark. He's engrossed in the match, oblivious to the turmoil in my mind. I should tell him. He would understand, offer comfort in that warm gentle way of his. But shame sticks in my throat like a lump of gristle. Mark knows only slivers of my past; fragments I could bear to share. The darker parts stay unspoken, buried deep. And that's the way I want to keep it.

I bring the mugs through, forcing a smile as I hand Mark his tea. He grins back, pulling me down on to the sofa beside him.

"You okay, beautiful?"

I nod, nestling against his shoulder. The familiar scent of his aftershave soothes my fraying nerves. I focus on the rise and fall of his chest, slow and steady, like waves lapping the shore.

"One of those days."

Mark kisses my hair. I close my eyes, letting the sounds of the match wash over me. As long as I have Mark, the ghosts can't haunt me.

"I need to pop out for a bit, forgot to grab something for dinner earlier."

Mark frowns. "We can order in a pizza or something?"

"No, I've got veg in the fridge that needs to be eaten, so I think chicken will go nice with that. I won't be long. You carry on watching the match and I'll be back before you know it." I peck his cheek and smile.

Before he can object further, I grab my keys and slip out of the front door. I drive on autopilot, my hands clenched tight on the steering wheel. I park up close to where I think I spotted David and start walking, my eyes scanning the passing crowds. It can't be him; I keep reminding myself of that. After everything he put me through, he wouldn't dare show his face again. I thought I saw him earlier, but maybe it was my imagination playing games with me.

I hurry along each street, ducking into cafés and shops close to where we drove earlier. I scan the sea of faces. They're all cheerful, unlike mine, which is tight and hot. My heart pounds against my ribs like a banging drum. I have to know if he's found me again. Exhausted, I step out of a bookshop and lean against a lamp post to catch my breath. Maybe I imagined the whole thing. David is not here, he can't be. I'm safe.

With a deep sigh, I turn and head to my car. Time to leave the ghosts behind. Mark is waiting for me.

As I dash back to my car, a breeze chills my clammy skin. I'm almost at the end of the street when a firm tap on my shoulder makes me yelp. I whirl around, pulse racing.

A tall figure looms over me, face obscured by the hood of his jacket. Fear spikes through me like shards of ice as I stagger back, keen to put some distance between us.

"Sorry, love, didn't mean to startle you," comes a gruff, unfamiliar voice.

The man steps back, revealing himself to be scruffy, middle-aged, and homeless. Relief floods through me. He shakes a tatty Costa cup in front of me. "Spare some change?"

I nod as I look around. My mouth is bone dry as I dip my hand in my pocket and pull out a few pound coins, dropping them into his cup. He smiles, tips his head, and wanders off, stopping a couple close to me.

"It's alright," I mumble, embarrassment heating my cheeks. Of course, it wasn't David. Why did I let my imagination run away with me? With one last glance around the busy street, I turn to walk back to my car, but I stop rooted to the pavement in horror. It's like my feet are stuck in a sea of glue and I can't move. Ahead, feet from me, a tall figure with familiar broad shoulders. I gasp, stumbling back against the shop window. It's him. David. Why is he here?

My mind reels in disbelief. He can't be here, not after all this time. But his cruel face is unmistakable. David covers the short distance in seconds, an odd smile playing about his lips.

Panic rising, I hold up a shaking hand. "Stop! Don't come any closer!"

To my surprise, he does as I say, raising his palms in a pacifying gesture. We stand frozen, separated by a gulf of pavement. Around us, shoppers flow past oblivious to the swell of panic rising within me.

"What are you doing here?" I struggle to keep my voice even.

David shrugs, an infuriating casual gesture. "I'm allowed to go wherever I wish, aren't you?"

My fists clench. How dare he act so nonchalantly after everything he did! But I can't lose control, not here in public.

"I don't want you near me." I grit my teeth. "You need to leave. Now."

His cold eyes flash with that familiar anger, but he simply inclines his head. "That's no way to greet your husband is it?" He smiles and laughs. "Oops, sorry ex-husband."

I stare after him. How can he be so calm, so collected, after destroying my life all those years ago?

"Jane." His voice cuts through the noise around us. "Funny running into you here. I'm around town often, doing my charity work, and I don't live far. You know, I've been hoping we'd have time to talk. There's so much I want to explain. Can we? I'd really like that. Honestly, there's nothing I'd rather do right now."

His final few words drip with sarcasm. Explain? Explain years of torment and abuse? I want to scream at him, but I know it will only cause a scene.

My stomach churns. "There's nothing to say. Please leave me alone."

He takes a step towards me, and I recoil. But David stops, holding up his hands again in a conciliatory gesture.

"No need to have a meltdown again. I've changed, Jane. Found God. He was my saviour. Helped me to see the error of my ways and put me on the right path. I admit, I was lost and terrible towards you, and I'm sorry, but I have moved on from that. These days I help the homeless and volunteer at a shelter. My lecturing days are over. I'm not the man I used to be."

My laugh is brittle and harsh. "You expect me to believe that?"

He cuts me off and interrupts. "Jane... really? Don't throw a wobbly. There's no need to take that tone with *me*." His cold voice deepens and tails off.

His dig infuriates me. "To trust you again?" My jaw stiffens in anger. "You're incapable of change."

David opens his mouth to protest, but I cut him off this time.

"We're done here. If you try to contact me again, I'll call the police."

Before he can respond, I turn and hurry away, putting as much distance between us as possible. My hands tremble and my heart hammers in my chest, but I don't look back. I can't let him suck me into his web of lies again. I duck into the narrow alley between two shops,

The Ex-Husband

pressing myself against the cold brick as I struggle to catch my breath. The world spins around me and I sink down, hugging my knees to my chest.

David is here. In this city, infiltrating this new life I've built for myself. The one place I felt safe and secure. But seeing him shatters that illusion, opening up old wounds I thought had healed.

I try to calm myself, to think rationally, but memories I've tried so hard to bury flood my mind. David's harsh words, his heavy hands, the sheer terror of waiting for the next attack. I've done everything to escape him, to start fresh. But now he's found me again, and I have no idea how that happened.

How long I sit there, paralysed by fear and anguish, I don't know. But finally, I force myself to stand on shaky legs. I have to get home. Have to tell Mark. He'll know what to do and keep me safe.

I head back to the car, and glance over my shoulder expecting David to leap out at any moment.

By the time I arrive home, my eyes are puffy and have a lattice of red lines, and tears streak my cheeks. Mark jumps up when he sees me, worry lines creasing his features.

"Shit, Jane! What happened?" He grips my shoulders as my body shakes with sobs.

"It's David. He's found me," I gasp out. "He's here. In Cambridge."

Mark's eyes widen in disbelief and fury. I hold onto him like a lifeline, refusing to let go.

5

MARK SETS me down on the sofa, his arm wrapped around my shaking shoulders. Though it's warm in my house, it feels like I'm sitting in an igloo as the hairs stand up on my arms and I shiver. My heart pounds as I recall everything that happened earlier.

"I thought I saw him across the street as we drove past. I couldn't be certain. It was a brief glance." My voice wavers. "When I looked again, he'd vanished into the crowd. That's why I had to go back. I needed to see for myself. I needed to be certain that my mind was playing tricks on me."

Mark's grip tightens. "And you found him?"

I swallow hard, nodding. "I searched everywhere and gave up, convinced it was someone who looked like him. I was heading back to the car, but then there he was, right in front of me."

"Christ." Mark runs a hand through his hair, worry etching lines on his forehead. "Why now, after all this time? What does he want?"

"I don't know." The old fear and panic rises in my

chest. It's taken years to rebuild my life after David destroyed it piece by piece. I can't go through that again. I won't.

Mark tilts my chin up, forcing me to meet his gaze. "Listen to me. I won't let him hurt you. Not again." His face softens with a small smile. "You're safe now. Do you understand?"

I nod, clinging to his words like a lifeline. With Mark beside me, I know I don't have to face this alone. Still, unease churns my stomach as I stare at the shadows gathering in the corners of the room as the light fades. Certain shadows linger beyond their time. David is one of them—and he's come back to haunt me. I take a shaky breath, trying to steady my nerves. "I thought I'd finally escaped him. That he was out of my life for good."

Mark nods. He brushes a strand of hair back from my face. "I know. But we'll get through this together."

Despite his reassurance, doubt claws at me. "What if he tries to take everything away again? My job, my home, you..." My voice sticks on the last word. After finding happiness with Mark, the idea of losing him fills me with dread.

"That won't happen." Mark's voice is firm. "He has no power over you now. You're not who you were back then."

I nod, but my hands tremble in my lap. Mark takes them in his, his calloused palms rough against my skin.

"You're stronger now. You rebuilt your life once before. If you had to, you could do it again. But you won't have to. Not alone." His gaze is intense. "I'll be right by your side, no matter what happens next. I promise. And if he tries to lay a finger on you, I'll kick his arse from here to the coast. He's not a man. He's a controlling and weak pussy."

Warmth blossoms in my chest, easing the icy fingers of

The Ex-Husband 31

fear. With Mark here, I feel like I can face whatever comes next.

"Thank you for everything."

He presses a kiss on my forehead. "That's what I'm here for. I love you, Jane."

"I love you too." The words fill me with strength. As long as we have each other, David can't touch us. He'll try, but together, Mark and I are strong enough to weather anything.

I LIE awake in bed long after Mark has drifted off. Sleep eludes me. My mind churns with unwanted memories of David. We met through mutual friends at the university where I worked. He seemed so charming at first, always ready with a compliment or a gift. The attention of a lecturer so intelligent and worldly flattered me. Too late, I realised it wasn't real love, but a way to control me.

I didn't see it coming.

The memories pierce like shards of glass. His scathing words when dinner wasn't ready on time. The way he'd squeeze my wrist until it bruised. How he cut me off from friends and family until he was my entire world. I shudder, rolling over to look at Mark's sleeping form. He looks so peaceful, his chest rising and falling in a steady rhythm. I reach out to touch him, then pull my hand back, not wanting to disturb him.

At least I escaped David's twisted version of love. Now I have the real thing with Mark. He makes me feel safe, not stifled. Cherished, not belittled. We bring out the best in each other.

When I started working as a secretary in the English department at the university, I was shy and unsure of myself in my new job, but David made me feel special right from the start.

He'd flash that charming smile and call me "love" whenever we passed in the hallway. During meetings, he'd make thoughtful comments on my ideas, as if what I had to say mattered. I'd blush and stammer, flattered by the attention of this handsome intellectual lecturer.

When he asked me to lunch in the café across campus, I was ecstatic. We talked for hours about books, art, and life. He was so witty and worldly, hanging on my every word.

After that, David bought me gifts—rare books he thought I'd enjoy. He'd insist on walking me to my car after work, opening doors and showering me with compliments. Each new gesture made me feel more cherished.

When he finally asked me out on a proper date, I said yes without hesitation. I was falling for David with dreams of our future together dancing in my head. If only I'd known then what darkness lurked behind that cultured facade. But my infatuation blinded me from seeing the truth. David had already captured my heart. The whirlwind fairytale continued, each date more romantic than the last. David would pick me up in his car, always dressed impeccably. He'd take me to gorgeous restaurants in town or plan cosy picnics by the lake. We'd sip wine, and he'd gaze into my eyes as he spoke of our beautiful life to come.

After a few months, he asked me to move in with him. I hesitated at first, worried it was too fast, but David insisted we were soulmates. He painted vivid pictures of waking up together each morning, reading by the fire at night. My reservations melted away. The day I moved in, David surprised me with a candlelit dinner. He dropped to one knee, velvet box in hand, professing his undying love and devotion. Too choked up to speak, I could only nod through joyful tears.

Our small wedding followed not long after. I wore a simple gown as we exchanged vows in the rose garden. We filled the reception with laughter, dancing, and hope for the future. As we drove away for our honeymoon, I never felt so full, so contented. I had everything I ever wanted— a husband who adored me and the promise of a beautiful life together. If only it could have stayed that way forever...

The honeymoon ended and real life began. At first, things were wonderful—lazy mornings in bed, cooking dinner together at night. But over time, David's moods changed. If dinner wasn't ready when he got home, he'd fly into a rage, shouting and throwing dishes across the kitchen. If I wanted to go out and see friends, he'd accuse me of abandoning him and not loving him enough, so I'd often cancel my plans. Bit by bit, he chipped away at my confidence, keeping me isolated.

The first time he hit me he seemed remorseful, blaming work stress. He bought me roses and my favourite chocolates to say sorry. I told myself it was a one-time mistake. But it kept happening. A slap across the face for a perceived slight. A punch in the stomach if I talked back. At night, he'd force himself on me while I lay frozen in fear and pain, praying for it to be over.

In the morning, it was as if nothing happened. He whistled while making coffee and kissed me on the cheek. "See you tonight, darling," he'd call out as he left for work. Meanwhile, I'd sit in silence nursing fresh bruises and soreness, my spirit growing dimmer each day. To the outside world, he was charming, helpful David, who loved helping everyone. No one guessed what he was capable of behind closed doors. I longed to run, but he'd threatened to kill me if I ever tried to leave. So I stayed. A prisoner in my own home, the walls closing in on my shattered dreams.

Mark's movement in his sleep jolts me back to reality. My eyes moisten as I sniff. I thought I'd run dry of tears, but there are years of pent-up sadness being held back by a crumbling and weak dam wall, and I'm not sure how long I can keep them at bay. I snuggle closer, reassured by Mark's solid presence. He stirs again, putting his arm around me. Comforted, I finally feel myself relax. The past can't hurt me any more. Not when I have someone like Mark by my side.

6

MONDAY MORNING, I sit at my desk, struggling to concentrate. Blinking hard, I try to shake the fatigue as memories of the weekend come flooding back. Sunday was a blur as I peered through the windows whenever Mark's back was turned. I wasn't sure what I expected to see, but the thought of David following me home niggled in the back of my mind.

I stayed indoors all day with Mark, who was adamant about not leaving me alone. By Sunday evening, the constant worry left me drained. Despite Mark's reassuring words, sleep evaded me most of the night. So I left for work early this morning while Mark slept, leaving a note telling him I love him and thanking him for his support.

With a team meeting on the agenda for this morning, my thoughts continue to race as I shuffle papers, unable to absorb the words in front of me. I know David. Nothing positive can come of his showing up after all this time. What does he want from me now? I rub my temples, willing my mind to settle, but it's no use. The image of his cold, blue eyes burn behind my eyelids, his words echoing in my ears. I have to pull it together before it eats me from the inside. I've been here before, and I remember how much weight I lost through fear, anxiety, and worry while being married to David and in the months after my escape and divorce. With sunken cheeks, ashen complexion, and dark hollows around my eyes, I looked like a corpse or an extra from a Halloween Horror Nights event.

My phone pings as I scurry to the meeting. Glancing at the screen, I see it's Georgia asking for a lunch date. I tap out a *Y xx* before heading into the room and taking my seat.

The conference room is stuffy, exacerbating my restless mind. I fidget in my seat, unable to follow the conversation as my colleagues drone on about overdue invoices, quarterly reports, and projections. All I can think about is David. Why now? After all this time, what could have prompted him to end up in Cambridge?

My pulse quickens as my thoughts spiral. Does he know where I live? Where I work? Has he been watching me? I dig my fingernails into my palms, struggling to steady my breathing.

"Jane?"

I jolt back to reality at the sound of my boss's voice. I meet his questioning gaze, realising all eyes are on me.

"Sorry, Brad, what was the question?" My face flushes a deep.

"I asked if you had the sales forecast ready for us to review." Brad studies me as his eyes narrow. "Are you feeling alright? You seem a little... distracted today."

I force a tight smile, smoothing my hands over my lap. "I'm fine. Didn't sleep very well last night. I'll have them ready to present after lunch."

My boss nods, though his eyes linger on me a moment too long before continuing the meeting. I try to refocus,

The Ex-Husband 37

pushing David from my thoughts, but his face and voice echo in my mind. I rub my temples as the meeting drags on, trying to ignore the dull pounding in my head. As soon as we're done, I hurry to the ladies and lean over a sink, splashing water over my face to cool what feels like an inferno breaking out over my skin. I look up at my reflection and shake my head.

I wait for a few moments, letting the redness in my cheeks fade before heading back to my desk, hoping to lose myself in the familiar routine of my work. But as I shuffle through the stacks of paperwork and files, my stomach drops. The quarterly sales reports I prepared last week are gone. I rifle through the folders again, panic rising in my chest. How will I explain this?

I'm meticulous with organising my work, always careful to check and double-check important documents are in their proper place. For them to disappear makes no sense.

Unless...

A chill runs down my spine at the thought, but I shake it away. I'm being ridiculous. It's a misplaced file, that's all.

I'm scrambling to recreate the missing reports over the next hour and have a little left to do when Georgia pokes her head in the door. "Hey! Still on for lunch?"

I wince, having already forgotten our standing lunch date. "Of course, sorry, it slipped my mind. Give me a few minutes to finish this up."

Georgia nods before leaving me to my frantic paperwork hunt. I feel awful, but there's no time to dwell on it. I have to pull myself together before I unravel. *You can do this*, I tell myself. Don't let David win. I try to focus. Time slips away as I recreate the missing sales reports from memory. My fingers fly across the keyboard, filling in tables and charts. The numbers and graphs usually give me a sense of control, but today they blur together. Out of the corner of my eye, I notice the clock ticking closer to noon. Georgia will be waiting for me soon. I'm almost done, a few more minutes.

My desk phone rings, jolting me out of my concentration. It's Rob from accounting, asking about the meeting room I'd booked for this afternoon.

"What do you mean it's double-booked?" I ask in confusion as I check my online calendar. I know I reserved that room weeks ago.

Rob apologises but says there's been a mistake, and now two different teams are scheduled for the same slot. My heart sinks, but I force myself to stay calm and polite as I thank Rob for the call and hang up. This day keeps getting worse. I rest a palm on my forehead as I place an elbow on the desk, trying to relieve the headache I feel coming on. First the missing reports, now this meeting room fiasco. What more can go wrong?

There's little I can do except beg another team to give up their room for my meeting this afternoon. But first, I have to face Georgia and my guilt over neglecting our friendship of late. My chair drags across the carpet as I push back with my heels and head out to meet her, determined not to let this anxiety and stress overwhelm me.

I head to the canteen, scanning the tables for Georgia's familiar face before I spot her waving from our usual table by the window.

"Hey, sorry I'm late." I slide into the seat across from her.

"No problem!" Georgia smiles as she closes the cover on her Kindle. "I know you're busy, so I ordered your usual. Hope that's okay. I've not been here long, but it gave me time to catch up with a few chapters. This thing is taking over my life." She waves her Kindle between us. "I tell you, since signing up to Amazon's Kindle Unlimited, my TBR list of ebooks has grown huge. I don't know when I'll find the time to read all these books."

"TBR?"

Georgia smiles. "To be read."

"Oh, right. Not heard that one before." I scoop up the cup. "You're the best, thanks." I take a sip of the chai latte she got me, comforted by its familiar spice.

"So tell me, how have you been? It feels like we haven't caught up properly in ages."

I hesitate, unsure how to answer. The truth is, I've been distant and distracted ever since I saw... him. But I can't tell Georgia about that, not yet.

"Oh, you know, same old." I keep my voice light and skippy. "The usual stuff, busy with work and Mark and everything."

Georgia shakes her head. "Come on, Jane. I can tell something's bothering you."

I shift in my seat. Georgia has always seen right through me. I consider brushing it off again, but the concerned look in her eyes makes me pause. This is Georgia, my best friend. If I can't confide in her, who can I trust?

"Well, okay. There is something. I saw someone from my past recently, someone I never expected to see again. It's... it's brought up a lot of complicated feelings. I'm still processing it all."

"Like what?"

I wish I could tell her, but shame clouds my thoughts.

Georgia pushes for an answer. "Good or bad feelings?"

"Oh, God, bad one hundred per cent."

"Come on, Jane. I'm here for you. Even if you can't confide in me, then who else can you turn to apart from Mark? Christ, I've told you a ton of shit in the past and getting it off my chest helped. Hey, it's me. You know I won't say anything."

I tighten as I splay my hands on the table, fighting the urge to snap, but it still overtakes me as I glance at her. My lungs squeeze the air out so I can't breathe, almost like I have someone sitting on my chest. "Sorry, Georgia, I can't. Can we drop it please?" I say as I fight the swell of panic rising in me.

Georgia sits back in her chair and stares at me open-mouthed, unsure how to respond.

I shrink inside, annoyed at my outburst. I hide my face behind my hands. I'm already embarrassed and angry with myself for everything that happened in my marriage. But at the time I didn't have the fight, courage, or self-confidence. I was scared of bringing further attention to myself and what David could do. Thoughts of talking about it publicly made me want to flee from the glare of the spotlight. To this day, the humiliation still hangs around my neck like a thorny necklace, stabbing at my skin and opening up fresh wounds.

"Shit, I'm sorry. I didn't mean to snap at you. I've hardly slept a wink all night. Forgive me?" I plead, burying my face in my hands as I gasp for air.

Georgia reaches across the table and squeezes my arm. "I'm here for you whenever you're ready to talk more about it."

I'm grateful for her friendship. "Thank you. Just being able to admit that much helps. I appreciate you looking out for me."

Georgia smiles. "Anytime. Now, drink up! We've got enough time for me to fill you in on Ardan's latest romantic antics before we have to head back."

Her stories always make me laugh, and the heavy weight on my chest lifts. With a friend like Georgia by my side, I know I'll get through this. I take a breath to collect myself. Seeing David again has sent my mind spinning, but I can't let it derail my life.

"You're right." I meet Georgia's gaze. "I can't let this distract me any more. It's in the past—I need to move forward."

Georgia nods and gives me the thumbs up. "That's the spirit. And you know Mark and I are both here for you."

"I know. Thank you." I'm truly grateful for her support. It bolsters my resolve. I won't let David worm his way back into my head and heart.

The server arrives then with our food, breaking the intensity of the moment. Georgia seamlessly switches gears, launching into a lively retelling of her boyfriend Ardan's latest romantic exploits. I laugh along with her story. The dark cloud over my head dissipates. As we finish up lunch, I feel centred again. I still have time left in my lunch hour to grab my coat to pop out for some fresh air.

As I step outside, the cold air helps clear my head after my conversation with Georgia. But as I head to the shops to grab some chocolate for the afternoon, the familiar tightness in my gut returns.

My eyes dart around, scanning every face in the crowd. Is he here watching me? I quicken my pace, hugging my coat tighter around me. Every tall man with dark hair makes my heart skip a beat. *Don't be ridiculous*, I tell myself. What are the odds he'll show up here? But my mind ignores logic, flooding it with "what ifs." What if he's been following me for days already? What if he's waiting around the next corner?

I feel myself spiralling, my breaths growing short and quick. No, I can't let the paranoia take hold again. With great effort, I force myself to take slower, deeper breaths. In through the nose, out through the mouth. In... and out. I focus on the rhythm of my footsteps, on the solid pavement beneath my feet. I am here, now, in this moment. Not trapped in the twisted games of my past. My breathing evens and my death grip on my coat loosens. The knot in my stomach unfurls.

This can't be happening again. I needed distance between myself and David, but it feels like I'm being pulled back into a world I thought I'd left behind years ago.

7

THE LAST FEW days have been terrible, and it feels like I'm stuck in reverse gear undoing everything I've built to shape my new life. I've caught glimpses of him all around Cambridge. He's always there, lurking, and going in the same direction I'm heading in or near the shops I need to visit. Coincidence or not, it's both bloody unnerving and terrifying. My heart races each time, a sickening dread washing over me that flattens my mood and sidetracks my thoughts.

I avoid my usual lunchtime walks with Georgia, citing too much work or deadlines looming. I feel bad for lying, and I hate to see the disappointment on her face.

Today is no different, as Georgia frowns beside my desk when I make another excuse to skip our walk. "You okay?"

I force a smile as embarrassment flushes my face, the memory of me lashing out at Georgia still fresh in my mind. "Just busy. I'm so sorry, but I promise to make it up to you."

She shrugs and doesn't push it any further as she

turns and leaves. I don't tell her it's David, because I don't want to worry her. But he's already there in my head, poisoning my freedom.

But even keeping to the main roads, he's there. Market Square, Corn Exchange, Grand Arcade. Wherever I pass, I see his face. But he always carries on past me, offering nothing more than a brief glance, his cold eyes meeting mine. It's not helping my nerves. I imagine his face around every corner now. My confidence weakens each day. I'm filled with a nameless terror and haunted in my city. He's winning again. And I don't know how to make him stop.

TODAY I DON'T HAVE a choice as I need to go into town to get my glasses fixed, so I stick to the main roads even though I know there are backstreets that can get me there quicker. I steel myself as I push open the door to Specsavers, clutching my broken glasses. The shop is busy, filled with people having eye tests in side rooms or picking out new frames towards the front of the shop. I wait to be seen, sinking into a hard plastic chair, my legs jittering with nerves, bounce up and down on my toes.

After what feels like an eternity, an assistant calls over to me and guides me to a desk. From her name badge, I can see her name is Samira, and she's friendly and efficient as she discusses the repair, but I can't focus as I chew on my bottom lip and glance out of the window.

"Is everything okay?"

I offer her a small smile and lie that I'm in a rush. Samira tells me it's a simple repair and shouldn't take more than twenty minutes so I can come back for them.

As I wait for my glasses, I escape next door to Star-

The Ex-Husband 45

bucks, hoping to blend into the crowd. I clutch my cappuccino in both hands, the heat warming my cold palms. With head bowed, I steady my breath, counting each inhale and exhale. I keep chanting silently that everything is okay. But minutes later, the hairs on my neck prickle and I glance up. He's here. David. Standing in line, now staring right at me. My chest constricts. I freeze like a deer caught in headlights. Before I can unlock myself from my static state and leave, he collects his coffee and makes his way towards me. I panic, thoughts racing. But there are people here. Witnesses. He can't hurt me.

False confidence propels me upright as he sits down opposite. "I didn't invite you to join me." My voice is strained but firm.

His eyes narrow. "Come now, Jane. We are two old friends having a chat. Don't tell me you've already forgotten that we agreed to catch up over coffee soon. Well, now seems as good as time as any."

I frown as confusion floods my mind. I don't remember that. "Please leave. I don't want any trouble." My hands tremble under the table and I feel glued to my seat. He leans back, regarding me with that smug, self-assured look I know too well. The one that still makes me feel so small and weak. It's the same smile he always wore as I cowered with my hands over my face, and he towered over me like a threatening menace.

"Trouble?" He laughs. "I'm not here for trouble, Jane. I want to catch up."

His casual tone unnerves me. I fight the instinct to look away, to appease. Instead, I meet his gaze.

"Why are you here, David?" My voice wavers despite my efforts.

He sips his coffee, pauses, and studies me with a smile before he glances round at the other tables. A small boy in a high chair catches his attention. David pulls a funny face and the boy chuckles in response, his mum throwing David an appreciative smile. He returns his attention back to me. "I'm allowed to visit an old friend, aren't I?"

I tilt my head to the side as I regard him. Did I just witness David being nice towards a child? He hates kids. "An old friend?" I repeat. "Is that what I am to you now?"

His eyes narrow again, a flash of annoyance passing over his features before the calm mask slides back into place.

"No need for the attitude, Jane. I'm extending an olive branch here as two mature adults. I'm sure *even* you can appreciate that? If we're going to be seeing each other around town, let's not ignore each other, especially after everything we've been through."

I lean forward as anger swells within me, and I hiss under my breath. "You don't get to reappear after all these years and act like we're old chums."

His jaw tightens. For a moment I see a hint of something else under the surface. But he smooths his features back into nonchalance.

"I was being friendly, my sweetheart. Thought we could have a civilised conversation." He shrugs. "But if you want to hold on to the past, that's your choice."

I draw in a deep breath to steady my nerves. How dare he call me sweetheart! He's twisting this around, putting the blame on me as always. "Civilised?" I repeat. "Was our marriage what you call civilised?"

David glances towards the ceiling and then returns his gaze to me. "Of course it was. Besides, that's in the past. I've changed and found faith to be my saviour. You should try it, it might help you. I've become a better person. John 1:9: 'If we confess our sins, he is faithful and will forgive us our sins and purify us from *all* unrighteousness.'" He

The Ex-Husband 47

pauses and then continues. "Matthew 6:15: 'But if you do not forgive others their sins, your Father will not forgive your sins.'"

I stare at him in disbelief. "Why the sudden change?"

David's face softens and for a moment, his features remind me of the gentle and loving man I fell in love with. He has the same look, and his eyes offer an attractive warmth that I once found appealing.

"You can't blame me for your mistakes which led to our marriage crumbling. I don't know what you're talking about. Sadly, you had the issues, not me. And I forgive you for those. I tried to help and support you. After all, you were my wife who I loved dearly, but..."

My anger spikes. "Don't pretend you've forgotten already. Does your newfound faith make it okay to put your hands on women?"

His mouth twists in a scowl. For a moment, I think he might lash out right here in the café. But he glances around, noticing the curious looks from nearby tables, and forces his expression neutral again.

"Keep your voice down," he mutters. "I didn't come here to fight with you. Same old Jane, hey?"

"Then why did you come?"

He sighs and leans back in his chair. "I told you. I've changed, found God, and now help people get back on their feet."

His tone is smooth, reasonable. I don't buy it for a second.

"Right. And working at the soup kitchen brought you back here, to Cambridge?"

David shrugs. "My faith led me here. Gave me purpose. And I found happiness again."

Anger swells inside me. "You don't have any purpose beyond your own ego. You haven't changed one bit."

His eyes flash with anger again. For a moment, I feel a twinge of familiar fear. But this time, I won't let him intimidate me into silence.

David's jaw clenches, but he keeps his voice low. "Look, I know things turned sour between us. But that was years ago—we were young, both at fault. I'm not asking you to forgive me right away. Just... give me a chance to show you I've changed. How the problems that crept into our marriage made me a better person."

He reaches across the table, as if to take my hand, but I pull away sharply.

"Don't touch me," I hiss. "I don't care how much religion you've supposedly found. You will never change."

His eyes narrow and he smiles. It's a dichotomy this man has perfected. "You always were stubborn. Never willing to see any perspective but your own."

"My perspective? You mean seeing my husband's fist flying at my face whenever you got angry? Having to hide the bruises from friends and family? So sore inside that I pissed blood?"

David glances around again, his jaw tight. "Keep your voice down, my dearest," he repeats.

"Why should I?" My anger is spiralling now, the coffee shop fading around us. "You don't get to waltz back into my life pretending everything's fine. I lived in terror of you for years—nothing can erase that."

David's mouth twists in a sneer. "Always so dramatic. You act like it was non-stop beatings. I barely laid a hand on you. You couldn't cope with being a wife. You didn't know *how* to be a good wife."

I stare at him, incredulous. Does he really believe that? Has he rewritten our past in his mind? I stand, my chair scraping against the wooden floor. "This was a mistake. Never speak to me again."

Before he can respond, I rush for the door, ignoring the curious stares around us. My hands shake, but my back is straight. I won't let him back in. Not this time. I burst out of the coffee shop, my heart pounding. The cold air hits my flushed cheeks as I gulp it down, trying to slow my breathing. I hurry away, keen to put distance between myself and that manipulative monster. Even now, years later, David still thinks he can justify his abuse and blame me for provoking him.

Waves of nausea scratch at my insides. David's presence in Cambridge makes my skin crawl. I chose this city precisely because it was far from our old life and from his influence. I worked so hard to build something new here. Now he's invaded this space too, tainting it with memories I've tried to leave behind.

My throat tightens as I recall all the times I tiptoed around him to avoid sparking his temper. The sleepless nights when he didn't come home, leaving me sick with worry. The way he chipped away at my self-esteem until I felt worthless. No. I refuse to let him back in my head. My life is different now—I'm different. I have a job I enjoy, good friends who support me. I don't need this shit.

Ducking into a doorway, I lean against the glass and close my eyes. My hands are still shaking. Seeing him brings it all back—the constant criticism, the manipulation, how he convinced me I was worthless without him. Even now, he thinks he can justify the abuse by blaming me. As if anything could excuse what he did, how he shattered my spirit. I'll never let him back in my head again.

8

I SIT at my desk unable to focus on work as I stare at my PC monitor. My mind replays the confrontation with David over and over. I swing from moments of anger to moments of dread. His smug expression and dismissive tone circle around my mind like a hungry vulture. How could he sit there and not accept responsibility for how he treated me during our marriage? He blamed me! He said it was my fault. How? What did I do to deserve blame for the bruises on my neck, back, inner thighs, and tummy? In what way was it my fault that I trembled in my bedroom, scared of how he would hurt me in bed? How? I didn't deserve to be abused so much that it hurt when I peed. The more I think about it, the more tense my body becomes. My shoulders ache, my eyes hurt, and it feels like there's a rubber band around my head, tightening its grip with each horrid thought that floods my mind.

I glance at the clock in the corner of my monitor again. Only fifteen minutes until I can escape to the sanctuary of home.

I rush through my front door, pulse racing, the keys jangling in my hand. After sliding the deadbolt into place, I lean back against the solid wood and take a deep breath before closing my eyes. The familiar surroundings provide a sense of comfort for my frayed nerves.

A sudden knock makes me jump. I peer through the peephole to see Mark's concerned face. I open the door and he steps inside, wrapping his arms round me in a comforting hug.

"What's wrong, babes?" he asks, seeing the tension lines creasing my forehead.

He follows me into the lounge where I sink on to the sofa. "I saw David today." I turn to Mark and see his jaw clench.

"Seriously? What happened?"

I explain the chance encounter in Starbucks, anger rising in my chest as I recall David's flippant and blaming tone. Mark listens beside me, his brow furrowed.

Mark takes my hand. "I'm so sorry, babes. I should have been there. But you're safe now."

I nod, attempting a brave smile despite the unease twisting my stomach. "You can't be with me twenty-four hours a day." I run my fingers across the back of his hand that's resting on my thigh as I try to clear the dark thoughts. "Tea?" I stand.

Mark pulls me back down. "Hey, talk to me. What do you need?" His warm brown eyes search my face.

I sigh, leaning into his solid frame. "I want to feel safe again. Seeing David brought it all back..." My voice trails off as images flash through my mind.

Mark's jaw tightens, a muscle twitching in his cheek. "That bastard. He won't get away with messing with you

The Ex-Husband

again." He runs a hand through his cropped hair in frustration. "I should find him and make sure he knows to stay the hell away from you."

I clutch his arm, my eyes widening. "No, Mark, please. That will only make things worse."

He searches my face as he narrows his eyes. With a heavy exhale, he pulls me close. "Okay, I won't do anything stupid. But if he lays a finger on you, I'll beat the crap out of him and wire his nuts to the mains before flicking the switch."

I cling to him, comforted by his solid presence. We stay entwined on the sofa as the light fades, drawing strength from each other. With Mark by my side, I can get through this. Straightening up, I look him in the eyes. "It's lovely that you want to protect me, but we can't do anything stupid. Without proof of harassment, the police can't do much."

Mark stays silent, but nods.

"He hasn't threatened me or laid a hand on me. As much as I hate it, he has done nothing illegal yet."

Mark drags a hand over his face, exhaling. "I know. I feel so damn helpless, Jane. After everything he put you through..."

His voice cracks with emotion. I reach up and cup his cheek. "I know. But we're in this together."

Mark turns his head and pulls me against his chest again. "Always."

I cling to him like a lifeline, tears pricking my eyes. We hold each other in silence as darkness falls around us. I breathe in Mark's familiar scent, willing my pounding heart to slow. He runs a soothing hand up and down my back.

"He can't hurt you again," Mark murmurs into my hair. "I promise I won't do anything drastic. But the second he tries anything, all bets are off. I'll cut off his nuts with my bolt croppers."

I nod against his chest. "Thank you. I want to get through this as calmly as possible." Despite everything, I feel the corners of my mouth lift in a small smile. No matter how dark things get, Mark always lightens the mood.

"I love you," I whisper.

Mark's arms tighten around me. "I love you too. So much."

I tilt my head up, seeking Mark's lips. He meets me in a fierce, desperate kiss. All our fear and anger collide, then give way to passion.

Mark's hands tangle in my hair as his mouth claims mine. My fingers dig into his shoulders, pulling him against me. We clutch each other like castaways in a storm, our bodies intertwined. Between hungry kisses, Mark murmurs my name reverently. His stubble grazes my cheek. My skin tingles everywhere we touch. We rip off our clothes piece by piece, our need for connection overwhelming. I drag my nails down Mark's back, and he groans into my neck. There are no barriers left between us. We move together in a steady rhythm, reaffirming our bond. Mark's gaze fills me with such emotion that my eyes moisten. We lose ourselves in each other, shutting out everything else. If only for these moments, it's us two again. No one can touch what we have.

I lay curled up on the sofa against Mark's side, our legs tangled together. His arm is draped over me as my head rests on his chest. I listen to the steady thump of his heart, taking comfort in its rhythm. My heart feels anything but calm. Though our lovemaking eased my anxiety, it still simmers below the surface. I can't shake the ominous feeling that David's sudden reappearance in my life is something more sinister.

What does he want from me after all this time? Has he been lurking in the shadows, watching and waiting to make his presence known again? The not knowing fills me with dread, and it's something I hate.

I feel Mark's lips press softly to the top of my head. "Talk to me," he murmurs.

I sigh, nuzzling closer against his warm skin. "I'm scared, Mark. David is unpredictable when he doesn't get his own way. And for him to show up now, after all these years..."

Mark's arm tightens around me. "He will not hurt you again."

I wish I understood what he's after so I could be better prepared. Mark trails his fingers up and down my back. "You should get some rest now, babes. I'll be right here all night."

I nod, exhaustion overtaking me as we peel ourselves off the sofa and head upstairs. Within minutes I feel myself drifting off, calmed by the steady rhythm of Mark's breathing. But as I close my eyes, I'm jolted back to full alertness. What was that? A tapping from somewhere downstairs. My body tenses. Mark must feel it too. His muscles stiffen. We both hold still, straining to hear any other sounds in the darkness. Another scratching noise, like nails on glass. Someone is trying to get in! I clench Mark's arm, my knuckles white. He puts a finger to his lips and eases out of bed, telling me to stay put.

I watch as he tiptoes to the bedroom door. He pauses there, listening, before turning the handle with excruciating slowness so the latch doesn't click, before slipping through the gap and disappearing from view. My heart hammers against my ribs. I reach for my phone off the bedside table in readiness to call 999. What if it's David down there, and he's come to attack me?

The wait seems to go on forever. I strain to listen out for any noise over the throbbing pulse in my ears. A yell splits the air and I bolt from the bed, race for the door, and charge down the stairs, screaming Mark's name. But his broad frame fills the hallway, blocking my path.

"It's okay," he pants, a little wild-eyed. "Just that bloody cat from next door clawing at the window."

Relief floods through me as we both shake our heads and let out smiles of relief.

9

MY HEAD POUNDS THIS MORNING. I don't remember falling asleep after Merlin, the cat, scared the living daylights out of me and Mark. I remember only staring at the shadows dancing across my ceiling as my mind raced in circles. As I sit at my desk, there's an avalanche of emails waiting in my inbox, but the thought of facing even one makes me groan. I can't face them. Not yet.

Two hours tick by in a haze before I drag myself downstairs to the canteen. I squint. The harsh fluorescent lights seem brighter than normal, and the chatter of colleagues from other floors drill into my skull louder than the sirens of a fire engine racing to a shout. I wince, shuffling to the counter to order a strong black coffee. The bitter aroma in the air is enough to revive me, if only slightly.

As I wait for my order and lost in my own world, I jump as someone pinches my waist and startles me. I spin round to see Georgia's grin, her eyes wide and teasing. But upon seeing me, her face takes on a seriousness as she studies my face.

"You look awful. Long night?"

"I'm fine," I mumble, avoiding her gaze. The last thing I need is her prying into my personal life again when I'm not ready to talk.

"Really?" she frowns, folding her arms across her chest. "Did something happen with Mark? You had a bust-up? Or is that person from your past still playing on your mind?"

My chest tightens at the mention of Mark's name, but for all the right reasons. I tilt my head, grab my coffee and turn away. "There's nothing to tell."

"Jane, you can talk to me." Her hand closes around my wrist, and I freeze in place. "We've been friends for years. I can see he's upset you."

I stare into the inky blackness of my coffee. Part of me is desperate to unburden the tangled mess of emotions twisting inside of me, but what can Georgia do? Nothing. If I tell her the truth, there's no going back.

"Please, Jane. I hate seeing you like this. You're my bestie. I'm not going to ignore the fact that something's up with you." She leans in and lowers her voice. "You're not pregnant, are you?" Her eyes widen as she searches mine.

After a long moment, I meet her gaze. "This has nothing to do with Mark."

Her eyes are soft, and the walls I've built up crumble. Before I realise, I'm taking her to a table away from everyone else to tell her what's been happening. The whole sordid story spills from my lips in a rush of words about my marriage, and David reappearing after I left to start a new life here, but I leave out much of the things he did to me. I can spare her those sad details. By the time I finish, tears streak down my cheeks.

Georgia reaches across and squeezes my hand. "Shit. I'm so sorry you went through that," she whispers, her voice heavy with emotion. "You deserve so much better."

"What am I going to do?"

"You're going to stay far away from that man." There's a firmness in her tone as she pulls her shoulders back to look at me. "He's manipulated you for too long. Promise me you won't let him back into your life again."

I nod, scrubbing the tears from my cheeks with the back of my hand. The thought of confronting David makes my stomach churn, and deep down, I know she's right. It's time I put myself first.

"I promise." A flicker of relief lights Georgia's eyes as she blows out her cheeks and smiles.

"Good. Now, do you want lunch? My treat."

The heaviness in my chest lifts. "That sounds good to me."

The canteen buzzes with chatter and clatter as I follow Georgia to the lunch counter. As we wait in line, she talks non stop, filling the space between us with funny work gossip and celebrity rumours, giving me a chance to collect myself. I'm grateful for the distraction. My nerves still feel frayed, my mind spinning with unfinished thoughts about David. I want to believe I can stand up to him now in a way I couldn't before, but doubts creep in. What if seeing him has awakened old feelings I thought were long gone?

We grab our food and settle at a table. As we eat, the conversation turns more serious.

"Have you heard from him since yesterday?"

"No. But I feel like he could turn up at any moment."

"You need to be prepared if he tries to contact you again." Her voice hardens. "He's hoping you'll let your guard down."

She's right. David excelled at finding my weak spots and exploiting them. I bite my lip, lost in thought as old memories resurface. Georgia reaches over, jolting me back.

"Hey. You got away from him once before. You can do it again."

I give my head a shake. "It's not that easy."

"Why?"

"Because unless you've been in a situation like that, you can't understand the impact it has on your mental, emotional, and physical well-being long after it's all over. It changes your identity. It changes who you become. You doubt yourself. You hate looking at yourself in the mirror. And you become suspicious about everything and everyone. Life is *never* the same again." I look away for a moment. As I glance around the canteen, I feel a disconnect from everyone. Like I'm not normal. Like I'm not part of the normal human race. I'm damaged. Mind and body.

"Shit." Georgia places a hand over her mouth. "I can't imagine what it would be like to be held in a relationship that bad. Was it...?" Georgia can't finish as her eyes moisten.

My body stiffens, steeling myself to open up.

"The control started slowly at first. He insisted on knowing where I was going, who I was seeing, and how much money I had in my purse. He didn't like me spending time with friends or family without him there."

I stare down at my hands, unable to meet Georgia's eyes. "When I didn't do what he wanted, he'd get so angry. Yelling, slamming things. I was terrified of setting him off, so I gave in." My voice drops to a whisper. "He hit me a few times. Never where it would show. And he always apologised after, said it would never happen again."

I look up at Georgia's face, her eyes wide and misty.

"Why didn't you tell me? I had no idea it was that bad."

I shrug. "He convinced me it was normal. That I was overreacting. I was too ashamed to tell anyone. Besides, I loved him. Love is blind and all that..."

Georgia reaches across the table to squeeze my hand. "You have nothing to be ashamed of. I'm so sorry you went through that alone."

Tears well up in my eyes. I gulp and keep going.

"When he showed up here, acting so kind... it threw me. He seemed genuinely remorseful. Like he wanted to make amends. Part of me wanted to believe he'd changed. He had a kindness in his eyes like I'd seen when we first met. It was one thing that drew me to him. I thought that perhaps there was still a bit of the old David that I adored still left in there."

I shake my head, hating that a part of me was swayed. "A small part of me considered trying to be friends. Proving I'd moved past it all."

Georgia frowns. "But you can't be friends with someone like that, Jane."

"I know." I lower my voice. "Logically, I know. But emotionally..." I trail off, struggling to describe the conflict within me.

Georgia shakes her head. "Abusers like him don't change. They're cowards and shitbags. It's all an act to reel you back in."

She's right, but I hate to admit it. "I know. Deep down I know. But he seemed so sincere..." Georgia grips my hand tighter.

"That's how they operate. He turns on the charm to get you to lower your guard again." Her tone softens as she leans into the table. "You're so bloody strong now. Don't let him unravel all the progress you've made."

A surge of newfound strength flows through me, a testament to the battles I've fought and won since leaving

David behind. The very idea of engaging with him now feels beneath me, a step back into a shadow I've since outgrown. "You're right. A small part of me considered we could be friends. Proving I'd moved past it all."

Georgia lifts one shoulder and lets it drop. "It's understandable to want closure. But you don't owe him anything. Not even a conversation."

Everything I hear makes sense, but it still doesn't sit well with me. I keep wondering if I'm strong enough now to not get sucked back in.

Georgia continues to push home her point. "Abusers are master manipulators. All those years together, he did a number on you psychologically."

Even as I listen to her, uncertainty flickers. He's in my head? Have I changed that much? Georgia seems to read my doubts and glances around to make sure no one is close by. She turns to face me.

"Jane. Look at me." Her gaze is fierce. "You are not weak. You survived him and built a new life. Don't let him fuck that up." She stabs her finger into the table with each word.

Her intensity startles me. But it's what I need to hear. I manage a small smile.

She tilts her head to one side. "Are you going to be okay?"

As doubts creep in, I still nod. "I think so. I need to stay occupied and not let it get to me or make me anxious."

"Easier said than done."

I let out a shaky laugh. "You're telling me."

We finish up and walk back to our desks, neither eager to end the conversation.

"Maybe we could meet up after work?" Georgia pauses

mid step and tugs my arm. "Go for a drink, or shopping, anything to take your mind off it."

"That would be great. I could really use the distraction right now."

As we reach my office, Georgia pauses by the door. "Call me if you need to talk more. About anything at all."

"Thanks for listening. And for caring. This stays between us, right?"

"Promise. And besides, what are friends for?" She pulls me in for a quick hug. "You'll get through this. I know you will."

I nod, blinking back sudden tears.

Georgia heads off with an encouraging wave.

10

A FEW UNEVENTFUL days roll by, and I feel a sense of relief that David seems to have taken the hint to keep his distance. Maybe I can finally get on with my life. But deep down, an uncomfortable feeling gnaws at me because I'm not sure if he's even still in Cambridge. I've not seen him around, but then again, I've tried my hardest to stay in the shadows and only go out when I need to, or when I'm with someone. My lunchtime walks with Georgia have been uneventful, which is a welcome relief. She hasn't pushed me about my past with David, and frankly, I'm tired of talking about it. Every time I do, waves of anxiety, shame, and humiliation crash over me as I dredge up memories I try so hard to keep at bay.

It's Saturday afternoon, and after spending the morning cleaning the house and changing my bedding, I head to Tesco to pick up a few bits. The car park is full, and it takes over ten minutes of driving up and down the rows before I find a space to squeeze into. And squeeze I have to as the car to my left has parked over the line to their bay and at such a stupid angle that I wonder how they passed their test. It's chaos, with no order and everyone out for themselves. I walk past a pair of motorists arguing about who had the right of way to take a vacant space.

"Oi! I was here first!" one shouts, her face red with anger.

"Too bad. You took too long to bloody move," the other retorts, smirking.

I grimace and hurry into the store, leaving them still arguing. Inside, I grab a shopping basket and weave through the crowded aisles, dodging shoppers left and right while making my way towards the fruit section. Tesco is packed on this busy Saturday afternoon, and I'm annoyed that I didn't come first thing. Crowds stress me out. I gather the first few items on my list—a bunch of bananas, a container of raspberries, and a bag of green grapes. But navigating the sea of trolleys proves tricky. I squeeze past an elderly couple examining the pears and sidestep a frazzled mum wrangling two small children who seem to do their best to annoy their mum, much to the amusement of other shoppers.

Escaping the chaos of the first few aisles, I head further into the store and as I turn down the baking aisle, I stop short. There, standing in front of the flour section and feet from me, is David. My heart leaps into my throat as he glances up and notices me. A smile spreads across his face and he walks over.

"Jane! Fancy running into you here." David's voice is jovial as if finding your abusive ex-husband in the supermarket is normal.

"Hello," I reply, clutching my basket tighter. Don't make a scene, I tell myself, though all I want to do is escape this situation as quickly as possible. "I need a few bits."

The Ex-Husband 67

Sensing my discomfort, David's expression softens. "Listen, I know things have been... difficult between us and you've let it get to you. But I want you to know that I have a new job lined up in Surrey. I'll be moving soon, so this might be the last time we run into each other."

"Really?" I can't help but feel the relief wash over me at the thought of David being out of my life for good. "Well, congratulations on the new job."

He smiles as he swaps a grip on his laden shopping basket. "Thanks. And before I go, I was hoping we could catch up sometime. Have a chat and try again to clear the air before I go? I appreciate that you're busy and it's the reason you forgot about agreeing to meet before. But it's a good thing that one of us is on the ball and isn't so forgetful."

My eyes widen at his arrogance. "I don't think that's a good idea, to be honest. There's a lot going on in my life right now, and I just... I can't."

"Jane, it would be a chat, nothing more," he insists, his tone softening. "We could meet in a public place. Once I move, you'll never have to see me again."

His reasonable tone triggers memories of how he used to convince me to doubt myself, leading me to question my judgment whenever I turned him down. A familiar anxiety creeps in and I need to escape. "Sorry, but I'm busy these days. Good luck with your move and new job, though." Before he can say anything else, I turn and hurry away, eager to escape. My heart pounds while I head to the checkouts, glancing over my shoulder. But David doesn't follow.

I let out a shaky breath as I load my groceries on to the conveyor belt, relieved to put some distance between myself and David. I know he can't try anything here because it's crowded. But seeing him still rattles me and I feel sick inside.

The cashier asks how my day is going. "Fine," I reply, forcing a tight smile. She makes small talk about the weather as she scans my items, but I only half-listen, eager to get out of here. I pay and gather up my bags before heading out to the car park. The sun is bright overhead, a warm spring day that now feels chilled. I walk, keys clutched in my hand like a weapon, glancing around for any sign of David. But I see nothing amiss as I glance around the rows of parked cars filled with families loading up groceries.

As I load the bags into my boot, I feel my pulse slowing. David didn't follow me out here. I'm safe. For now, at least. But the encounter leaves me rattled, a reminder that he's still lurking nearby, despite my hopes that he left for good. I slide into the driver's seat and lock the doors at once. As I start the engine, I decide—I need to call Anita. I've kept this all to myself for too long already. It's time to open up to my closest friend about what's been happening. Anita needs to know about the return of my worst nightmare disguised as my ex-husband. She'll know what to do. I pull out of the parking spot and head for home.

I pull into the driveway and lug the groceries inside, eager to unload my burden. As soon as my hands are free, I grab my phone and dial Anita. She answers on the second ring.

"Jane! How are you, love?"

Her warm, familiar voice puts me at ease. "Oh, Anita, I'm so glad you picked up. There's something I need to tell you."

I launch into the whole sordid tale, starting with seeing David in town. Anita listens, letting me get it all out

The Ex-Husband   69

in a jumbled rush. When I finish, she's silent for a moment, but I can hear her sucking in breath.

"What! I can't believe this." I sense the anger creep into her tone as she continues. "After everything he put you through, now he's back to interfere in your life again? Unacceptable."

I let out a shaky breath, beyond relieved to have shared this with her. "I'm scared, Neets. He has this power over me, even now. I freeze up whenever he's around."

"That's understandable after the shit you went through. Listen, let me check my diary and book a train ticket. I'm coming to Cambridge to see you. We can catch up and talk. He doesn't get away with that."

"Thank you. I've missed you so much." My voice is nothing more than a whisper as I fold one arm round my waist.

"Me too, love. I need you to hang in there."

I sigh as my shoulders sag. "When he approached me in Tesco today, it felt like I was transported back to the past. All the old feelings of doubt and intimidation came flooding back."

Anita makes a sympathetic noise. "He's a manipulator. Don't let him make you question yourself."

"I know. But he was so calm and reasonable, going on about wanting to explain himself before he leaves town. Some of me wishes to believe he's changed, and I want to hear him out." I give a hollow laugh. "Pathetic, right?"

"Not at all," Anita reassures me. "You have a big heart. But a leopard doesn't change its spots. David is toxic, and you need to protect yourself."

"I panicked and got out of there as fast as I could. In my hurry I didn't even get half of the things I needed. I'm such a coward."

"No, you did the right thing. Don't beat yourself up,

babe. Now we can come up with a solid plan to keep him away from you for good."

I nod, determination rising to replace the fear and self-doubt.

"I'm so thankful, Neets." My voice cracks with emotion. "I was spiralling into that dark place after seeing David. It felt like all the hard work with my counsellor was beginning to unravel."

"That's what friends are for. Now, tell me what he said to you so we can analyse his game."

I recount my interaction with David, cringing at how easily I slipped back into my former placating and appeasing mode. Anita listens, making the occasional grunt of disgust and tuts loudly. "Unbelievable. He expected you to meet him for coffee? So he could explain away his abuse? Not a chance." Neets' firm stance reassures me as a small smile breaks on my face. There are times I wish I was more like her.

"I know. But I felt paralysed, as if I couldn't help but be civil with him."

"You've got nothing to apologise for. I say we front him out and show we're not scared of him, or we go to the police and get a restraining order."

The suggestion makes my stomach twist into knots. "I don't know... We don't need to provoke him. He has done nothing wrong, and he's been mostly pleasant."

"Jane, listen to me. You have done nothing wrong here. David is the one who needs to be put back in his place. I've done it once to him, and I'll do it again if I have to. First things first—documentation. We need evidence in case this escalates further. Keep records of any contact from David. I can also be a witness to his past harassment if needed."

I listen as Anita rattles off everything I need to take on

board. My mind spins. She's like a sergeant major in the army barking orders at their troops. No wonder David backed down when she was there to defend me in Norfolk. Anita helped me to escape and find strength and belief in myself. Without her, I'm certain I wouldn't be alive today. We hang up not long after, and for the first time in a few days, I feel stronger.

11

THE COFFEE MACHINE splutters and gurgles, pouring hot brown liquid into my chipped mug. It's no way near as good as what's served in the canteen, but I don't fancy traipsing downstairs to get one. This tar-like looking liquid will have to do, but I wonder what it's doing to my insides by the way it sticks to the walls of my mug. I clutch it, savouring the warmth seeping into my hands, and take a deep breath. The familiar aroma calms my overactive mind as I shut my eyes for a few seconds.

After my call with Anita last night, I woke with renewed energy and purpose, bouncing into work with, dare I say it, a small skip in my step. Clive and Abnash were already in and arguing about a free kick or something in a game they'd watched at the weekend. But upon sitting at my desk and firing up my PC, a sickening knot forms in my stomach. As I open my drawer, the Randel account quotes and drawings have vanished from my files. I search every drawer and cabinet close by, nothing. Shit. My breath comes faster and faster. How could they disappear into thin air?

Abnash spots my frantic rummaging. "Everything all right, Jane?"

Panic tightens my throat as I draw in a sharp intake of air. "The Randel quotes. They're gone."

He frowns and joins me, looking over my shoulder as I rummage through every scrap of paper on my desk. Nothing. Abnash calls out, "Has anyone seen the Randel account quotes or drawings?" Everyone shakes their heads. Of course not. If they had, this wouldn't be happening.

Abnash squeezes my shoulder. "Are you sure you didn't misfile them? A load of files went down to the archives in the basement. Could they have got caught up in those?"

"Positive." I bite down on my teeth and quickly scan my workspace. "Right there is where I filed them." I gesture towards the empty Randel file in my drawer. Anger and frustration churn my insides. First the sales reports and now this. My mind spins in circles struggling to make sense of it. I always prepare everything carefully, filing each document in its proper place. So how did they disappear? It doesn't make any sense. I wiggle my mouse and then search for the Randel folder on my system. The folder is there, but it's empty. Did I delete the contents by accident? But I check, and there's nothing in my recycle bin either.

My eyes widen as I look at the screen. What have I done with them? Unless... I glance around at my team, a chill running down my spine. One of them must have taken the files and deleted the folder as they have access to it too. But who? And why? No, that makes little sense. I'm being ridiculous for even thinking about it. Maybe in my frazzled state I wasn't thinking straight and deleted it by accident. But it would be in my recycle bin if I'd done that. This makes little sense.

Abnash steps closer, lowering his voice. "Try not to worry. We'll figure this out."

I sigh as I realise that I'll have to pull the data together again and recreate the documents.

As I slump forward in my chair, I open my emails to check for any updates, and a new message catches my eye. It's sandwiched between two others I've already read. How did I miss it earlier? My eyes narrow as I click it open. There's no sender name, only a random string of numbers and letters from a Hotmail account. The subject line reads "Secret Admirer".

I scan the brief message, my breath catching in my throat.

My dearest Jane,

I've been watching you from afar, longing to tell you my feelings, but I'm a little shy. You're stunning and I'd love to get to know you. Hopefully, our paths will cross real soon.

Yours always,

Your Secret Admirer

My hands tremble, almost knocking over my coffee mug. Who sent this? And how did they get access to my work email? I read the message again, and a chill spreads through my veins, unsettling me. This is no simple prank or case of mistaken identity. Is this a wind-up? Is someone toying with me? But who? And why me? I minimise the window so no one else will see. I don't feel safe here any more. I glance around the office again, suspicion gnawing at my core. Someone in this room is playing games with me. I need to figure out who.

I tut and curse, then head up two flights of stairs to the IT department. I make my way to Kiran, the closest support team member. I use the term "team", but it's two guys who appear bored whenever I'm there, and Kiran is the only person I talk to because he's friendlier than Winston.

Kiran closes one of his two screens, bolts upright in his chair, and shifts as I approach, his eyes never leaving me. "Hi, I need help to trace an email." I give him the details of my account and wait for him to pull up my records. He leans into his screen and avoids too much eye contact with me. I look over his shoulder as he studies files I can't make heads or tails of.

Kiran frowns as he finds my records and looks over the data on his screen. "Hmm," is all he says to begin with.

"Is that it?"

"I can try to trace the IP address, but if they used a proxy server or public network it will be difficult."

I nod, biting my lip. He runs a few searches and then shakes his head.

"No luck. The origin remains unclear. I'm sorry."

My shoulders slump in disappointment. Of course it wouldn't be that easy. "Nothing else you can do?"

He shrugs a shoulder. "We only offer first line support here and it's mainly network and hardware stuff. Techprompt, an external managed services company, handles all our server, backup, and software support. I can drop them a line?"

"While you're doing that, can you ask them to locate some files that somehow got deleted?" I ask, closing my eyes in frustration and nodding in reply. "Maybe they can retrieve them from a backup?"

"Sure, give me the details." Kiran pushes paperwork to one side and searches for his yellow Post-it pad and jots down the details.

"Thanks, Kiran. You've got my work mobile, so call me when you have something for me."

The Ex-Husband

He nods. "Sure. No problem."

As I head back to my desk, my thoughts turn to David. Could my manipulative ex-husband be behind this cruel prank? It would be like him to mess with me, even after our divorce. I have no proof, but the toxic dynamic of our relationship makes him my prime suspect. David always got a kick out of keeping me off-balance and in a constant state of unease. This sinister email has his fingerprints all over it. I wouldn't put it past him.

My hands clench into fists. I vow to remain vigilant. I won't let this so-called admirer—whether it's David or someone else—intimidate me.

"JANE, WHAT'S WRONG?" Georgia asks as we sit down to lunch.

I sigh, poking at my salad with my fork. "I got a strange email this morning. It was sent through the company server, but from an unknown address. Said I had a 'secret admirer'." I do air quotes.

Georgia's eyes widen with excitement. "Oooh, a secret admirer! Looks like Mark has competition!"

"It's not like that. The email creeped me out. I asked IT to trace it, but they couldn't find the source."

Seeing my distress, Georgia's expression softens. "Oh, honey, I'm sorry. I was only teasing. That sounds unsettling."

She reaches across and squeezes my hand. "Any idea on who sent it?"

I bite my lip. "I wondered if it could be David, trying to mess with my head again."

"Ugh, that would make sense. Wouldn't put it past him." Georgia frowns.

I grip my fork. "I can't prove it, though. Could be anyone. I can't think of anyone in the office who'd send that. It's too creepy."

Georgia reaches for me from across the table. "Well, don't you worry. It's probably a harmless prank."

The suggestion does little to quell my paranoia. "Maybe, but why say they've been watching me from afar? Are they stalking me? Is that person out there right now?" I jab my fork towards the window.

"What about Olu, in the post room? He's flirted with you, and it's bloody obvious he has a soft spot for you."

I wave off her suggestion. "He's harmless and wouldn't harm a fly."

Georgia tuts. "It's the quietest ones you need to watch out for."

I nod, though my stomach is still in knots. Who is behind this? First the missing or deleted files, and now a creepy love note.

As I dash back to my desk after lunch, I feel uneasy, as I scan the room and look at my colleagues typing away at their computers. Any one of them could be messing with me. Sitting down, I force myself to focus on the work in front of me. But the questions keep swirling in my mind. Did David send that email to torment me? Or is someone else playing twisted games?

My cursor blinks on the blank document I opened to redo the Randel quotes. But the words won't come, my thoughts consumed elsewhere. I shake my head to dislodge my spiralling speculation. No use driving myself crazy with paranoia. I have a job to do as I type up the quote details again. The answers will come in time. For now, I need to stay focused.

12

I SIGH, my fingers hovering over the keyboard for a moment before hitting "send" on the last email of the day. The relief is real and feels good as I log off the computer. So many things have gone wrong today, and it's a day I want to forget. I rarely make a mistake at work, and yet a few have happened in the space of only a few days, and even as I sit here now waiting for the screen to go off, I have no answers why.

"Jane!" Georgia calls out, her voice jolting me from my reverie. She and Clive stride over to my desk, both looking eager to get out of the building. "We're going for a drink; you should come with us."

"Not *a* drink!" Clive shouts. "Several. And the bigger the drink the better, so make mine doubles and you're paying!"

I smile. "Thanks guys, but I'm not in the mood," I answer, hoping they won't press any further.

"Aw, come on, Jane," Clive insists, his eyes pleading. "We've not seen much of you lately. I'll tell you what. I'll buy the doubles and you can get the singles. You can't get fairer than that, right?"

"Really, I appreciate the invite, but I can't tonight. Besides, Mark is coming over for dinner." My voice wavers, letting slip the anxiety simmering beneath my facade.

Clive opens his mouth to push again, but Georgia cuts him off, pushing Clive towards the lifts. "Leave her be, Clive. It's fine, Jane. We can do it another time." She glances over her shoulder and gives me a sympathetic smile. "But if you need someone to talk to, call me, okay?" she whispers out of Clive's earshot.

"Thank you," I mouth back, grateful for her understanding, leaving me to gather my things in silence. As I pack up my bag, I can't shake the feeling that something is so wrong—a nagging sensation that something doesn't quite add up. But no matter how hard I try, I can't ignore it.

The vague email from this morning replays in my mind as I go home. Even after spending hours agonising over it, I still can't make sense of who sent it or what they hoped to gain. Could it be someone from work trying to unnerve me? Or is it David, finding a new way to get at me even though he doesn't have my email address?

My head throbs upon stepping through the front door, the day's stress compounding into a fuzzy mess. Right after placing my bag down, the phone rings, the shrill tone piercing the silence.

"Hi, Jane, it's Kiran from tech support. Sorry to bother you but you asked me to bell you when I had an update. I've been down to your floor and one of your colleagues said you'd left, so as you'd given me your moby, I thought I'd call you. Hope that's okay? Anyway, I wanted to let you know that before I left for the evening, Techprompt hadn't located the missing files you reported this morning."

My heart sinks as I suck in a deep breath. "What? Seriously? Are you sure?"

"They've searched the drives and backup servers, but there's no sign of them ever existing."

I grip the phone tighter, trying to steady the urge to scream in frustration. How could those files simply disappear? I didn't imagine them. Something isn't right here. "Okay, thanks for the update."

"Hey, listen, I couldn't help but notice you seemed stressed and anxious when you came to see me. Is everything okay? Has something happened?"

"Um... yes. I've got a lot going on at the moment."

"Okay. Is there anything I can do to help? Anything?"

Despite his kind words, I don't think anyone can help me. "Honestly, I'm fine. But I appreciate the offer."

Kiran goes quiet for a moment. "Well, I'm here if you need me."

I thank him. As I end the call a wave of dread washes over me. What is happening? My thoughts race while I attempt to understand it all. But no matter how I look at it, nothing adds up any more. I take a deep breath to calm myself as I hear the front doorbell ring.

I swing the door wide to find a cheerful-looking Mark. When he's like this, he reminds me of a market trader with all the lines and cheeky smiles.

"Hey, gorgeous." Mark leans in to kiss me.

I force a smile even though it's hard to be cheerful. "Hi. Good timing, I'm starting on dinner. How's ham, egg, and chips sound?"

"One of my favourites." Mark's eyes light up at the mention of food as he whips off his coat and hangs it on the newel post before following me into the kitchen. "I swear that little café by my work does ham, egg, and chips like yours."

I nod, already lost in thought again as I crack the eggs into the frying pan. Mark chips in and helps as we get the simple meal together, then takes our plates to the small kitchen table. As we eat, Mark chats on about his day while I push the food around my plate, unable to take more than a few bites.

I feel his eyes on me, his brows knitting together in concern. "Are you okay? You seem quiet tonight."

"Hmm? Oh yeah, just tired," I reply with a weak smile, avoiding his gaze.

An awkward silence settles between us. I stare down at my plate, knots twisting in my stomach. My thoughts race as I try to make sense of everything, wishing I could tell Mark what was troubling me. But without proof, I don't want to concern him over what might only be paranoia. So I keep pushing my food around, lost in my spiralling thoughts, while the silence hangs heavy over our table.

Mark reaches across the table, placing his hand over mine. "Did David try anything today?"

"No, nothing at all."

Mark studies me for a moment before giving my hand a gentle squeeze. "You know you can tell me anything, right? I'm here for you, always."

His brown eyes are full of warmth and concern. I feel a pang of guilt for not telling him about the strange email and my missing files, but what is there to say when I don't understand it myself? I can't imagine Mark could shed any light on it either. David's always been Teflon-coated, slipping through the cracks with ease. Outside of our house, he was golden, adored by all. With no evidence, it's always been my word against his and Prince Charming always seems to come out on top.

The Ex-Husband

"I know, and I appreciate it." I manage a small, grateful smile. "Just one of those days, you know?"

Mark nods, though his eyes flick from me to his plate and back again. I change the subject to his work, and he launches back into lighter conversation, which is a relief for me. His hand stays clasped around mine. The contact is comforting, keeping me tethered amidst the mass of my dark thoughts though I hate hiding things from him. I know mentioning my suspicions now will only make him feel powerless and angry, and the last thing I need is Mark charging round Cambridge to hunt down David. And I hate to imagine what would happen if he got hold of him. For both our sakes, I have to stay quiet until I have proof of what David is up to. The not knowing is agonising, but I don't want to drag Mark into this mess unless I'm certain. I need to hold on a little longer.

After dinner, Mark heads upstairs to shower while I busy myself cleaning the kitchen. The mundane tasks of loading the dishwasher and cleaning the table and dinner mats usually calm my nerves, but tonight my thoughts race unchecked. With Mark occupied, I grab the chance to go around the house checking the locks on the doors and windows. My fingers fidget as I test each one. I know it's irrational, crazy even—we live on a quiet street on the outskirts of Cambridge, and David doesn't even have my address—but I can't help it.

Finally, I peek through the living room curtains into the dark and empty street. Not a soul about. The stillness is eerie, as if the world is holding its breath. I search the shadows, expecting to see David emerge at any moment from the darkness. Of course there's nothing, not even a lone cat or fox. Just my overactive imagination tormenting me. With a shaky sigh, I let the curtains fall closed.

Upstairs, I take a quick shower, the hot water doing

little to unwind my tense muscles. After changing into pyjamas, I slide under the duvet beside Mark. He smiles, throwing his arm over my chest, oblivious to my turmoil. I close my eyes, willing my racing thoughts to stop, but that image of the email keeps coming back. "Your Secret Admirer." But who? It has to be a wind-up.

David's face flashes into my awareness—his cold blue eyes and cruel smirk. My pulse pounds as I imagine all the ways he could torment me from afar. Beside me, Mark's breath deepens into sleep. In the small hours of the morning, I give into the exhaustion, but David's face still haunts me even in my dreams. I toss and turn, the sheets tangling around my legs. Shadowy visions plague me—faceless figures lurking, David's icy stare, messages appearing on my computer screen. I jerk awake with a gasp, heart hammering.

Beside me, Mark stirs. He rolls over and lays a comforting hand on my arm. "Hey, you okay?" His voice is gravelly with sleep.

"Yeah. Just... bad dreams."

Mark squeezes my arm. "Wanna talk about it?"

I hesitate. I don't want to stress him out. "No, it's okay. Go back to sleep."

But Mark props himself up on one elbow, his brows furrowed in concern as he rubs his eyes and yawns. "Come on, something's bothering you. I can tell."

My throat tightens. His steady gaze is so earnest, so caring. Before I can stop myself, the words spill out—my worries about David, the missing documents, the malicious email.

Mark listens without judgement, his fingers tracing soothing circles on my wrist. He waits for me to finish before saying anything. "I know it seems scary right now, but I won't let him hurt you. The email probably came from someone at work who fancies you."

Tears prick my eyes. I don't deserve this man.

Mark pulls me close, and I cling to his hairy chest, breathing in his familiar scent. The steady thump of his heart calms my own racing pulse.

"Try to sleep," he murmurs. "I'll be right here all night."

13

I'VE TAKEN annual leave from work and wait patiently at Cambridge train station. Following the turmoil of the last few days, I'm really looking forward to Anita arriving to stay with me for the night. She's the conduit to my old life back in Norfolk, but for all the right reasons. I pace around the concourse glancing up at the information board every few minutes to check for the latest arrival times. Anita's train is on time and only a few minutes away.

With the last of my coffee drained, I throw the paper cup in the nearest recycling bin before folding my arms across my chest as I wait. Daily life goes on around me. Students mill around checking their phones before glancing up at the information board. Workers are darting through the turnstiles heading off to work, and retirees are passing through, pulling small cases on their way to somewhere nice I hope.

If only life were this simple. Apart from the recent years spent rebuilding in Cambridge, it's been a constant uphill battle. I know my childhood was good. Though I was quiet and shy, I was often happy with my own company. Going to university brought me out of my shell, though I still clung on to a few of my introverted ways. And for most of my life I've had a habit of saying "I'm sorry" more often than I should. I guess it became worse after I married David. That phrase became part of my everyday vocabulary. It was easier to become more passive and non-confrontational, internalising my stress rather than showing it, because it would only antagonise David further.

Despite being in a safe area, I look over my shoulder and check my surroundings. The email from yesterday has really spooked to me. Everything seems okay, but then I spot a man leaning against the wall near the doors. His eyes keep moving from me to the information board behind me. A shiver runs through me as I move from where I'm standing to get closer to the attendant who is checking tickets near the barrier. At least here I can feel safe.

The man doesn't give off a troubled vibe, but his constant glances in my direction make me uneasy. He looks to be in his mid thirties, wearing dark jeans, white T-shirt and a blue denim jacket. After checking the information board again, I see Anita's train has arrived. I shift my attention towards the doors again, and he's no longer there. I check up and down the concourse. He's not here. I don't know whether to feel relieved or concerned. I don't have time to think about it as a familiar voice echoes across the concourse.

"Janie!" Anita shouts as she marches with purpose through the barriers with her arms outstretched, one hand still clutching her Kindle. Anita is my best friend from Norfolk and seeing her makes me smile. She hasn't changed. Anita is a striking black woman in her late thir-

The Ex-Husband 89

ties with long braided hair done in cornrows, and big warm brown eyes that are glistening as she approaches me. She's always had a knack for making a statement. With her bohemian style of fashion, her extrovert personality, and her colourful language, she is not someone you can miss.

"Oh my God, it's so good to see you, chicken." Anita's booming voice draws the attention of others around us. But I doubt she even knows as we are lost in our own blissful world of tight hugs that leave us gasping for breath. I close my eyes and welcome her warmth and embrace. She is taller than me and shapelier, so it feels like I'm in a wrestler's bear hug. Anita finally lets go and takes a few steps back, casting her eyes up and down as she studies me. "My Lord, woman. You've not been eating much have you? There's nothing left of you. Lord have mercy on you!" she shrieks, slapping her Kindle against my arm. "We need to get a plate of jollof rice in you." Anita sucks in air through tight lips and fans her face as if we are standing in thirty-degree tropical heat.

I close my eyes and laugh. Anita is so much like Mark. Even in the depths of my despair, they have a knack for lifting me. "Come on, let's get you back."

I PUT the key in the door and step through, carrying Anita's overnight bag. Anita follows, her eyes wide as she studies my small lounge. She coos, making animated gestures with her hands as if she stepped on to the stage and is entertaining the audience.

"This is cute. What you're missing is my final finishing touches. It's drab and dreary in places. You can tell I had no part to play in decorating this place."

I throw my keys on the table and head into the kitchen and flick on the kettle, batting off her teasing. "Tea or coffee?"

"Are you serious, girl?" Anita stands in the doorway to the kitchen, hands on hips. "Spiced rum, baby!"

"Neets, it's only gone eleven. We can have a drink later on." I point at the kettle, prompting her for an answer. She huffs and chooses coffee.

I make our drinks and together we drop on to my sofa and enjoy the comfortable silence between us for a few moments as we sip our drinks and stare at each other. As much as I would love to stay here and sit in silence, I know Anita is waiting to hear about everything that's been happening. And it doesn't take her long to get to the point.

"So, are you going to tell me what the fuck has been going on?"

Where do I start? Because it feels as if I have so much to tell, but I start at the beginning when I first spotted him in town, to when I bumped into him in the supermarket, before touching on all the things that have gone wrong at work and the dodgy email.

"I don't get it. He had the entire country to move to. Why Cambridge?" Anita questions while sipping her coffee and staring into space.

I haven't got an answer for her, and all I can do is shrug. "He claims it's a coincidence, and that he is a changed man. He keeps pestering me for a coffee because he wants to explain everything before he moves to Surrey to start a new job."

Anita jabs a finger in my direction. "Listen to me, he is a dangerous man. Regardless of whether he claims it's a coincidence, I don't buy that bullshit. He has done nothing by chance or accident. He has always planned everything. David planned on being here!"

The Ex-Husband 91

I sink back in my chair and close my eyes. "This can't be happening again."

"The first thing you need to be concerned with is your safety. Make a note of every time you come across him. If he's loitering close by, take a photo. Send everything to me so we have a backup copy in case you lose your phone. We need evidence in case we need to take this further." Anita points a finger at me. "He thrived on manipulating you and everyone else around you. David is bloody good at it. He's a saint out there." Anita jabs a finger towards the street beyond my lounge window. "But he is a dangerous bastard behind closed doors. And no one ever saw that apart from you, and any other poor woman who fell for his charms."

I shrug. I've fallen for his charm and his words a thousand times despite my resistance. Even now there's a magnetic pull towards David I can't explain. So much of me wants to put as much distance as possible between us, but there's a tiny part of me that is still connected to him. He was a man I loved. I gave him everything, mind, body, and soul. It saddens me he used that to his advantage, and by then it was too late for me to get away.

We spend the rest of the day dipping in between conversations about how to get David off my back, my relationship with Mark, my work, and her life back in Norfolk. Just hearing her talk about everything happening back home leaves a heaviness inside as it tugs on my heart. The fact I still call it *home* after everything that happened takes me by surprise. And by the time evening comes along and I'm preparing her bed in the spare room, it feels like there is no space left in my head to take in anything else. But one thing is certain, we need to speed up David's move away from Cambridge.

FOR THE FIRST time in a few weeks, I sleep well. Maybe it's because Anita is here, or perhaps because it feels so cathartic to get everything off my chest. Anita helped me to escape from David's clutches. We planned for weeks how we could distract him, which would give me enough time to get away. Over the course of a many weeks I *threw away* a few of my clothes, only for Anita to fish them out of the bin in the dead of night. More and more of my personal possessions left the house through that route, so that when I left him I had everything I needed.

I want to show Anita around Cambridge, so we decide to grab a brunch in town and have a mooch around the shops. Being a Tuesday, the streets are quiet compared to the last time I was here with Mark. It makes it easier for us to stroll and talk. I tell her more about my life in Cambridge, how much I'm enjoying work and the sense of freedom I feel. Well, the sense of freedom I *felt* until David showed up. Anita tries to gloss over that last fact by reminding me he'll be gone soon and will be nothing more than a distant memory.

Of course, she's right, but it doesn't stop the fact that he's reawakened the memories of my time with him. Though I don't tell her, there's a battle raging inside my mind. How can I hate him and love him at the same time? He hurt me in every way possible, but each time I see him, I'm reminded of how it felt to be wrapped in his arms, to feel his lips on mine, and to be lost in the passion that we once felt.

We stop at a café, and though it's not a warm day we decide to sit outside while we both have eggs florentine and coffee.

"Thank you for coming." I place the knife and fork down and take a sip from my coffee.

"How could I not? My best friend is going through shit, so what kind of friend would I have been if I didn't come over as soon as I could?"

And I appreciate it. I must've told her a dozen times last night and it still doesn't seem enough. It feels like she's my safety blanket and though I want to stay positive, the doubts already creep back into my mind about how I will cope when she's gone.

I'm about to pick up my cutlery again when I glance over Anita's shoulder and freeze. David is walking towards us, glancing around him as if out on a casual stroll. He spots me and smiles as he slows down. "Shit!" I mutter.

Anita pauses and stares at me, a look of concern breaking out across her face as she narrows her eyes. She glances over her shoulder to see what I'm looking at before stiffening. "What the hell?" She jumps to her feet and stands between me and David, blocking his view. "Stay away. Don't you think you've done her enough harm already? You come any nearer and I'll call the police."

Taken aback, David glares at Anita, but raises his hands and remains composed at Anita's show of defiance. "Good to see you after such a long time, Anita. I wasn't aware you were here." He looks over her shoulder towards me, his face lifeless and cold.

There's no love lost between them, and I know how much David despises her for what she did.

David smiles, his face non-aggressive as he takes one step back. "I'm heading to the shops and not looking for trouble, so enjoy the rest of your day." He sidesteps Anita with a curt smile and throws me a cursory look as he walks past. David's smile disappears as he stares at me, his jaw clenched. It's that look I've seen thousands of times.

An angry stare in response to someone talking back to him. My body stiffens, fixed in the seat and unable to move as I hold my breath, waiting for him to pass.

Anita waits for him to disappear before taking a seat again. "Bastard," she hisses. "He thinks he's so special."

My chest sinks as I let out a deep sigh. I know Anita is being tough, but I can see a hint of fear in her eye as she stares after him. It's clear that he's rattled both of us and suddenly, I've gone off my food. I rest my elbows on the table and hide my face in my hands. Why won't this stop?

Anita reaches out and squeezes my arms. "Hey, listen. I'll always be by your side, no matter what David is up to. He won't bother you again."

I peek at Anita through the gaps in my fingers as a small tear rolls from my eye. As much as I want to believe her, I think Anita might have made it worse.

14

THE REST of the day goes by in a blur. I'm not in the mood to carry on window shopping, and I'm terrified of bumping into David again. Deciding that we only have a few hours left together, we head back to the safety of my house. While Anita packs to head back to Norfolk, she reassures me that everything will be fine. I only wish I shared her optimism, after all I'm the one left behind.

We settle on the sofa for a final cuppa. There's not much else to say that hasn't already been said in the past twenty-four hours. It feels like we're going over the same ground again. I guess it's Anita's way of hammering home the facts that David is moving on soon and I can pick up the pieces once again. She means well, and I appreciate everything she has done for me, but I don't know how much fight I have left in me. Seeing David leaves me feeling exhausted each time. Any exchange of words between us only makes it worse because those conversations keep swimming around inside my head.

When it's time to say goodbye to Anita, I take her back to the train station. It's a goodbye I don't want to have.

"Hey, listen, I'm only a phone call away. I'm sorry I couldn't stay longer but I'm already behind in my work. How about if I come down in a week or two? Maybe make a long weekend of it?"

I nod and cling on to every word she says like my life depends on it. "The sooner the better. I know I'm asking a lot of you, and I've got friends here, but you and I have been through so much together and without you I wouldn't be in Cambridge. They don't know the history like you do."

Anita hugs me and kisses my cheek. "You did all the hard work and got away. I helped a little. Just a bit." She draws her thumb and forefinger together with a little gap in between them.

I glance up at the information board before giving her one last hug. "Go, your train is leaving in a few minutes. Text me when you get back home."

She gives me one final squeeze. "I will."

And with that, Anita heads off through the ticket barriers, shooting me one last look over her shoulder before disappearing around the corner and on to the platform. Once again, I'm all alone, even though there are at least another dozen people milling around on the concourse.

———

SINCE I DON'T HAVE to go into the office today, my house feels silent without her. It's as if I'm missing a favourite piece of furniture, and things don't look right. Mark's busy working, as is Georgia, so I'm alone with my silent ruminations. I make myself a cup of tea and decide to keep myself busy by cleaning down the kitchen worktops and washing the tiled floor. The thought of watching a movie

The Ex-Husband
97

on Netflix appeals, but I know I won't be able to concentrate, and it won't be long before *those* thoughts crowd my mind.

I tackle the lounge next, pushing my Hoover into all the nooks and crannies, moving sofas, hoovering up the dust that seems to have settled on the top of the skirting boards, and I even discover the odd small cobweb in one corner of the ceiling. Another hour passes. Surprisingly, I've done well to keep myself busy.

There's still a bit of tea left in my mug, so I blitz it in the microwave and cradle the mug between both hands while I wander over to the lounge window to see what's happening in the big wide world beyond my house. I don't spot it right away as I look down the street, but I'm soon left speechless as my mug hovers an inch from my lips. David is further along the street talking to my neighbour Chrissy.

"Shit, he's found out where I live." I grab my phone and take a photo of David. How? Questions flood my mind. He must have followed me at some point. Did he tail me from the station after seeing Anita off? How long has he known that I live here? My jaw trembles through the familiar fear that floods my veins. I open WhatsApp and send his picture to Mark and Anita with a text. I've done well to keep him at a safe distance, but he's here now! In my street! "Leave me alone, you bastard!" I hiss, before placing my mug on the windowsill and rushing to the door.

I throw it open and march with purpose, almost breaking into a run, as I race down the street towards Chrissy's house. David and Chrissy are in deep conversation, both of them laughing at something they've shared.

Chrissy sees me approaching and waves. "Jane, lovely."

I stop beside them, out of breath, as I glare at David. "Stay away from my neighbours and me. Stop harassing them. You have no right to be here. Did you follow me?" The words spew from my lips as I jab an accusatory finger in his direction. "Why are you doing this?"

Chrissy seems horrified by my reaction as she stands there open-mouthed.

David offers a sickly sweet smile at me. "I'm here to help, but behaviour like that can lead to unforeseen consequences, so I'd be careful if I was you." With that, David turns and crosses the road, heading towards his car.

My heart thuds in my chest as I watch him go. Every muscle in my body wants to chase after him and rip the skin from his face. How dare he come here to my street, to where I live?

"Jane, love. What was all that about?" Chrissy's voice carries concern as worry lines crease her forehead.

"Um... Well... He is not good news. I've had a run-in with him before." I try to find the right words to not alarm her, but what I want to say is that he is a dangerous, sadistic, manipulative, and toxic person.

Chrissy pulls a face. "Are you sure? He seems a lovely chap. He is visiting all the elderly residents in the local area on behalf of the church to see if there's anything he can do to help folks like us. I was listening to the charity work he does. He comes across as a very thoughtful, caring, and considerate person. We could do with more people like that in this world."

I want to say to Chrissy, "Don't be fooled by all that bollocks," but I would come across as a twisted woman who has lost the plot.

"Jane, lovely, you shouldn't talk to people like that. That was quite rude of you. You know, he even offered to drive me to church on Sundays or pick up groceries for us.

The church is about salvation, and he's a perfect example of someone who puts other people's needs first."

Chrissy's praise for David churns my stomach. She's being won over by the same charm that once swept me off my feet. "I know what you're saying, Chrissy, but you don't know him like I do. He's not who he claims to be," I say, my words a sharp warning cloaked in calm.

Chrissy bats off my concerns. "Nonsense. I bet that man hasn't an evil bone in his body."

I blink hard as I glance at Chrissy. Is she talking about the same person? Of course she is, but this is what David does best. He charms everyone around him, so they all think he's a saint. I could talk to Chrissy until I'm blue in the face about what David is really like, and it would be me who comes across as looking like the rotten apple.

David sits in his car and stares at me. He is doing this to intimidate me, and yet there's nothing I can do. I can't call the police and tell them that my ex-husband is sitting in a car close to my house and staring at me. I know what David is like. He will wave those church pamphlets in their faces and tell them he is doing a good deed on behalf of the church, and they will believe him.

Then I realise David is strategically turning my friends and neighbours against me with his charms. He is positioning himself to come out of this looking as the saner one between us, with me becoming more unhinged as each day passes. All these things that have been happening only add weight to how people see me.

I storm back to my house, with Chrissy still blabbering in the background about how I shouldn't judge people. I'm seething and terrified at the same time. He's started again. Bit by bit, eroding my life. David watches me, a satisfying grin on his face as I pass him.

Pushing the key in the lock, I stumble through my

front door in my haste to get back inside. I slam the door behind me. My body shakes as I pace around my lounge with my arms wrapped around me before returning to the window and staring through the net curtain at David's car. I'm glued to the spot, expecting him any minute to step back out and approach my house. A few minutes later I hear his engine rumble into life, and he pulls away from the kerb, disappearing down the street and out of view.

Uncertain about my next move, I chew on my bottom lip. Hopelessness is weighing on me. I'm not with David any more but am I going to get him out of my life once and for all? Is he leaving Cambridge, or is that another lie? Even if he leaves, what is there to stop him from coming back to stalk me? I shut my eyelids and grit my teeth as I see a vision of me thrusting a knife into his chest when it all becomes too much, and I snap. But that's not like me. I don't like violence and I hate confrontation. The times I have come face to face with David have been out of desperation and as a last resort to save myself from another beating, but it's clear now that my words have little effect on him.

As I stand on the precipice of a decision, my heart battles between despair and a desperate hope for freedom. Can I ever escape David's shadow, or am I destined to dance on the edge of fear, forever looking over my shoulder? With each haunting thought, the line between survival and surrender blurs, pushing me closer to an ever-desperate choice, and it's one that I know I need to make on my own.

15

IT'S BEEN a few days since Anita left and though we've spoken on the phone a few times, I still miss seeing her. Mark has been amazing and has stayed over every evening after work so that I'm not alone. He knows that David was in my street talking to Chrissy, and even though I didn't want to tell him, it felt like a violation. My home is my sanctuary. My safe place. It doesn't feel that way now. David knows where I live.

Thankfully, he has kept his distance. Though it hasn't stopped me from peering through my windows and scanning the street every night for anything out of the ordinary. For all I know, he could lurk in the shadows, and I haven't spotted him. But his apparent absence from my neighbourhood hasn't stopped the tightness in my chest every day. I have to admit I have seen him around town while I've been on errands during my lunch hour. Georgia has been with me, and I've pointed David out to her. She's not as feisty as Anita, and favours caution over confrontation, ushering me away in the opposite direction every time we see him.

Today is no different. I'm able to slip away not long after being at work to run to the post office for stamps. It's Anita's birthday in four days and I'm a little late in getting a card for her. Although I should have given it to her in person, a first-class stamp should deliver it to her in two or three days.

I remove a stamp from its backing and stick it to an envelope before dropping it in the box near the post office. I remind myself to order flowers for delivery and to call her on the day. As I turn around to head back to the office, I let out a scream that catches the attention of passers-by.

David is in front of me. He holds his hands up so that everyone around him can see that he poses no threat. *If only they knew.*

"Sorry, I didn't mean to scare you. I was heading back towards the church to drop these booklets off. There weren't many takers today, so I ended up with spares." He waves a handful of thin brochures in front of me that have a picture of a church on the cover.

I take a few steps back, eyes wide with concern. "What do you want?" I feel safe here knowing that he can't do anything in public.

David smiles. "Nothing. I'm packing up, and I didn't expect to see you again. How about if I buy you a coffee and we can talk? If after ten minutes you don't want to listen to any more, you can walk out, and I won't bother you."

There's a gentleness in David's voice that I haven't experienced in many years. I often heard it in happier times when we used to sit across the table at our favourite restaurant, each with a glass of wine, his hand resting on mine. We would stare into each other's eyes, lost in our own dizzy, loving world. It was so intense that it sounded

The Ex-Husband 103

like the noise of conversations around us was nothing more than a mumble.

But that gentle tone soon became a trademark of how he spoke to me after he assaulted me. He would cradle me in his arms, brushing the hair away from my damp and bruised face before running a finger along my jaw and gazing into my eyes. He always told me how much he loved me, and how sorry he was. He'd say that I made him do it. By the next morning he'd be whistling with a bright cheery grin on his face as he waited at the table for me to make his coffee and breakfast.

His head tilts to one side. "Please?"

It takes a while before I nod and agree. I'm not sure why. It's like a part of me is pulling me in a direction that I don't want to go but I can't help it.

We head to a café across the street where he orders us two cappuccinos. I decline his offer of a pastry or cake. It's an awkward silence between us to begin with. Though I sense I'm far more nervous than he is. He is disarmingly casual, slouched back in his chair, casting his eye around the different tables.

The cappuccinos arrive and David thanks the waitress before waiting for her to leave. I wait for him to take a sip of his coffee before I say anything. It's like a piece of me longs to find out more answers and fill in the missing pieces to what I already know.

"Why have you appeared in Cambridge after all these years apart? You had the whole country to choose from. Why here?"

David takes in a deep breath and licks his lips as he ponders my question. "I've moved a lot and once found myself in a Manchester church, deep in thought. Being in a peaceful personal space had a profound impact on me, but I can't explain why." David stares at the ceiling, the corners of his mouth curling up. "I recall grabbing a leaflet from a nearby chair. It spoke about Christ. I won't bore you with all the details, but there were a few powerful statements about living your life, seeking forgiveness, and opening your heart to love. And from that moment onward something changed inside me. It just clicked."

I sit and listen, almost dumbstruck. This is the first time I've ever experienced David speaking like this. The suspicious part of me wonders how much of this is true. Has he changed?

"My faith led me around the country until I ended up meeting a lovely lady at a church event in London and she was from Cambridge. Well, close to Cambridge. She invited me to come and visit and I fell in love with the place... and her."

It's my worst nightmare when he mentions a village where they live. It's minutes from me.

My eyes narrow into slits. "I've heard your lies repeatedly. This is more of them."

David shakes his head. "Jane, believe me. I know you've heard me say this before. And I know it sounds corny or cheesy. But I've seen the error of my ways. I've developed a passion for helping those less fortunate."

I frown as I narrow my eyes.

David sighs and nods. "We've both moved on with our lives. Our relationship and marriage were toxic, and that wasn't good for either of us."

I grit my teeth and clench my fists under the table, unsure if I've heard correctly. Toxic?

Leaning forward across the table, I glare at him. "The marriage wasn't good for us? I did nothing to you. Have you forgotten what you did to me? Has it slipped your

The Ex-Husband 105

mind how you inflicted mental and physical cruelty on me?" Venom courses through my voice.

"I've not forgotten... what you made me do," he replies maddeningly calmly. "You were emotionally unstable and defaulted to playing the victim, almost as if that became your identity. Despite my efforts to get you the help you needed, you refused. The doubts and paranoia took hold of you and as each month and year passed, I lost more of the woman I loved. So I have to question the reliability of your memories."

I choke on my saliva. My mind spins with what I've been told, but before I reply, he continues.

"I am sorry for whatever you think I did, and I beg for your forgiveness. And if I could turn back the clock and do things differently, I promise you I would." He reaches into the inside of his jacket pocket and pulls out a picture, turning it around to show me. "I'm a father now. This is my little boy, Freddie. He's three. I've turned my life around. With my background in IT, I now work as an IT infrastructure manager for an IT services company and I'm building a future for Freddie and my partner, Siobhan. She's a nurse at Royal Papworth Hospital."

I stare at the picture of the young boy as David continues to tell me that Freddie has started nursery. Freddie looks a happy and bouncy little boy who is grinning from ear-to-ear in the picture as he holds up his favourite toy. I look at David who's smiling like any proud father.

"He's a smashing little boy. Full of beans and a mummy's boy. He never ceases to amaze me, and I notice something new about him every week. They grow up so quick." He shakes his head in consternation.

My chest tightens and a wave of nausea churns my stomach as a sweaty sheen coats my forehead.

"Once we move to Surrey and are settled, Siobhan and I plan to try for a little brother or sister for Freddie."

My mouth runs dry as I try to swallow down the bitter bile that scorches my throat. The suggestion that they're going to try for another child stings. Every muscle twitches with the desire to throw my cappuccino all over him. Why is he punishing me still? He hated the idea of children when we were married. What's changed in him? Was I that much of an unsuitable wife and potential mother? Was I nothing more than a punchbag for him? There are so many questions swimming round my mind that they drown out David's words, and all I can see are his lips moving.

I take a while to come back in the room and to what he's saying. It feels like I'm in a parallel dimension.

"I hoped that this could have been us, but we weren't right for each other." His voice is harsh and cutting. He always had a knack for sticking the knife in and kicking me when I'm down. He glances at the time on his phone and then drains the last of his drink. "I must go. I'm running late. Jane, please think about it. I'd like it if we can be civil. All I'm asking for is forgiveness."

I watch as he buttons up his jacket and rises, offering me a small smile before heading for the door and leaving me shell-shocked. My mind struggles to process everything I've heard. Did I dream it? How could he have said all those things and blamed me for all of it? What did I do wrong?

From the moment we met, I loved everything about David. He was charming and intelligent and respected in the lecturing community. I used to feel proud to be his wife and be on his arm when we attended university events. He commanded a certain aura and power with his presence. As a senior lecturer, they held him in high

The Ex-Husband 107

regard, almost mythical status, and he would turn heads wherever we went.

Pain grips my insides as they twist. Seeing the picture of Freddie leaves me choked. It was too much to listen to. How could he? How could he talk about Freddie and the prospect of another child after everything that happened and what he put me through? What about my loss? What I suffered at his hands is something that haunts my dreams most nights, and I want to run and hide every time I see a child in a pram.

I rise from my chair, my body numb, and my senses in disarray. A lone tear spills from my eye and snakes its way down my cheek as I shuffle between the tables to the door. I'm oblivious to those around me as I bump into chairs, ignoring the tuts and angry stares.

16

GETTING into Jane's home was an important part of my plan to get closer to her and taking the five-day locksmith course was the best £1500 I've spent. Who knew there was so much to learn about the different aspects of UPVC doors and multipoint locks, right through to mastering pin tumbler mechanisms, cylinder key identifications, mortise locks, and using pick guns? It means I can gain access to pretty much every home regardless of the locks they have on their doors. Obviously, I can't access properties with alarms, but I know that Jane's house doesn't have an alarm.

Crouching down by the back door to her property, I take less than ten minutes to find the right pick tools to unlock the mortise locks on her rear patio door. I push down on the handle and open the door a few inches, placing my ear closer to the gap and listen for any noise.

As I thought, no one is at home. I know Jane is at work. Pushing the door, I peer through the gap as it becomes wider, revealing the kitchen. Lingering smells of coffee hang in the air as I step inside and spend a couple of moments to familiarise myself with the layout of the ground floor. It's a clean and functional kitchen. No signs of dirty plates or pots tossed into the kitchen sink. It's spotless as I run my finger along the worktop looking for dust. Nodding in approval, I go from the kitchen to the through-lounge with dual aspect windows facing both the front and rear.

I fill my senses with the familiar aroma of her perfume. When I shut my eyes, I can briefly picture myself beside her, burying my nose in the curve of her neck and taking in her fragrance. I can feel the softness of her skin against mine as I kiss her neck. My arms are wrapped around her small waist as I pull her body in closer to mine. I can hear her gasp at the suddenness. I wish she was here now.

With nothing for me to do down here yet, I head upstairs to her bedroom. It's the bigger of the two, with the small bedroom only having a single bed for guests. As I make my way into Jane's bedroom, I'm surrounded by everything that reminds me of her. I run my hand down her dressing gown which hangs on the back of the door before making my way over to her chest of drawers, opening each drawer and running the tips of my fingers across the fabric of her underwear, her tops, then her silky pyjamas.

Stepping over to her bed, I lift her pillow and press it against my face, closing my eyes as I breathe her in. Placing the pillow back down, I smile to myself and wonder how she would feel knowing I had violated her inner sanctum. Would she freak out at the thought I held her underwear in my hands or curled a few loose strands of hair around the tip of one of my fingers? Probably. I guess at this point she would throw up.

As much as I'd like to stay here, I have work to do. I

remove the rucksack from my back and place it on the floor. I'm going to leave her a few surprises. One for her bedroom, the bathroom, lounge, and kitchen. I'm not sure she'll find them straightaway; I doubt it very much. She is clever, but not that clever.

I want to know everything she does. Every move she makes. And every private moment she has.

This is about control.

My control.

And Jane needs to be doing what I need her to do, so I can have her forever.

17

MY BODY IS tense from the shock as I take the elevator up to my floor, pushing through the glass doors and heading towards my desk. Clive looks up and smiles, and I throw him a small smile in return. Conversations are being played out around me, colleagues are talking on their phones, and there's the familiar clickety-clack of keyboards, but with my senses dulled it feels like I'm underwater.

As I drop my bag on the floor beside my desk, I slump into my chair and stare at my blank computer screen. David's words still sting as my mind replays our conversation on a loop. Did he say all those things, or did I imagine them? My mind is in disarray, and I question how much more of this I can endure. I go through days where I am determined to make this stop, convincing myself that he'll be gone soon, and I can rebuild my life again. But then there are days like this where I question if I can pick myself up.

My shoulders sag with exhaustion, and my mind feels like there isn't enough room in there to think. Tension stiffens my shoulders and neck. It's as if a vice is squeezing the muscles and restricting the blood flow to my head as it pulsates in rhythm with my heartbeat.

Why is he doing this? Or perhaps I should ask what is he doing? He hasn't laid a finger on me, nor has he said anything vile. Yes, some of his words have been hateful and worrying. And perhaps that's the clever game he is playing. I can't rush to the police saying that my ex-husband has been saying nasty things to me. I'd come across as nothing more than a little girl in the playground rushing to her teacher and saying, "Miss, David is being horrible to me!"

There is so much to unpack from that conversation. But I guess the picture of Freddie hurt me the most. I dreamt of being a mum more than anything else but every time I raised it with David, he refused point-blank to discuss it or even entertain the idea. His career was too important to him, and the responsibility of children was an imposition on his life. And he went to great lengths to tell me I wasn't mother material.

I blink a few times and try to concentrate. It seems as if I've been gazing at this empty screen for hours, but it's only been a few minutes when I wiggle my mouse to wake the screen. With a heavy sigh and the prospect of having to refocus on a million things on my to-do list, I check my emails in case there are any important requests that need to be actioned first.

I scan through the first few. Nothing major and I can tackle those later this afternoon. The accounts team is asking for an update on any recent invoices that they're not aware of yet. I scroll past all of those. It's the next one I come to that catches my breath. My jaw drops and my eyes widen in a mixture of surprise and shock. It appears to be another anonymous email and the prospect of opening it fills me with a black dread.

Knowing I have no choice, I open the email and scan the brief message, absorbing each word one at a time before going back to the beginning and starting again.

The reality is that you will grieve forever. You will not get over the loss and you will not learn to live with it. You won't heal and rebuild yourself, nor will you be whole again.

Glancing up from my screen, I look around my team. Who sent this? Could it have been someone internally? There are over seventy people in this building across four floors. I recognise most by face. But I can't think of anyone who would send me something like this. I print a copy off and race up the stairs to the next floor to see Kathy Shields, the HR and Operations Manager. Kathy's door is open, and she's shuffling through paperwork as I appear in her doorway.

"Kathy, have you got a moment?"

She glances up and greets me with a warm smile. We've chatted a couple of times, mostly in social settings, and from what I've gathered about her, she is empathetic. "Sure, come in. How can I help?"

"This feels awkward. I've received two anonymous emails. The first wasn't too bad. A bit of a love note from a secret admirer, apparently. The second which I received today has left me unnerved." I hand the sheet of paper to her.

She takes a few moments to read it before looking up at me. "This is quite distressing. Do you think it is someone within the organisation?"

I respond with a shrug. "I'm not sure. Kiran in IT

couldn't find the source of the first email, so I doubt he can trace this one either."

"I have to ask, but have you had any difficulties with another member of staff, or been involved with anyone here?"

"No. I get on well with everyone."

My nerves twist inside me and I chew the skin around my thumbnail.

Kathy nods as she thinks through her response. "Okay. I take things like this seriously. This comes across as both malicious and harmful. I'll speak to Kiran and our IT outsourcing partners. I'll also reach out to the police to make them aware if that's okay with you?"

"Thank you."

"I have to ask, but is there anything going on with your personal life outside of work? A former partner or friend that you don't get along with any more?"

I want to nod. Of course there is. David. If I spill the beans, I'll only be seen as a crazy woman with wild theories and accusations, but the more people who know, the better it is for me. My stomach spins like a Catherine wheel and I feel the heat rise to my neck. What will she think? Will I sound like a pathetic, sad woman who let her husband control and beat her? Stopped her leaving the house? Decided who she could talk to? What she should wear? I feel shame as I swallow hard and wince as bile torches my throat.

"Yes, there is something. David, my ex-husband from Norfolk, has appeared in Cambridge and I've bumped into him a few times." As guilt courses through me and stiffens my muscles, I pause. As I shake my head and cast my eyes downwards to the carpeted floor, I feel a rush of embarrassment that causes my cheeks to blush. I grit my teeth at how I've allowed David to control my life for so long. "It was an abusive marriage, and I escaped to start a new life."

"I see. I'm sorry to hear that." Kathy reads the message again. "It sounds quite personal. Perhaps something that happened in your life that resulted in you suffering a loss? Does anything like that ring a bell?"

"Yes. I lost a baby during our marriage." I pause, grit my teeth, and close my eyes. "He forced me to have a termination."

Kathy apologises with a warm smile as her tone softens. "I know this is difficult. Do you think David may be behind this email?"

I shrug as I wipe the moisture from the corner of my eyes. My heart feels heavy, and I swallow hard to push down the tightness in my throat. I worked so hard with my counsellor to overcome the PTSD I experienced after escaping. With her help, I thought I had worked through the painful memories of the abuse and control, and of my termination, but mentioning it again has brought back the profound feelings of loneliness, guilt, and anger I once felt.

"Okay, leave it with me, and I'll get back to you as soon as I have more information. If you receive anything like this again, get in touch with me straightaway."

I wrap my arms around my chest and thank her for her time before leaving. As I'm heading back to my desk, I stop in mid step. I know it's him. I don't know how. But David is behind it. My mind races. What if he is the cause of all the problems at work? The missing reports. The double-booked rooms. Did David do those things too? Hastily, I rush back, grab my bag, and sprint towards the exit. I ignore the look of concern on the faces around me as I rush past them.

RACING TO THE CHURCH, I park my car and slam the door with a force that shakes the glass. I march towards the church entrance and head straight to the small shop where David works. He's finished serving a visitor and is about to serve a couple when I barge right past them, my face full of fury and my body rigid with anger.

"You sent me the email, didn't you? How bloody dare you!" I shout.

David takes a step back, his eyes shifting between me and the next customers. "I'm sorry. I do not know what you're talking about. Please, this is a place of peace, and I don't want you upsetting visitors to our church."

Every ounce of me wants to scream and let out all the pent-up tension in my lungs. "I don't care. You know what you've sent. You know the loss I suffered. A loss that was *your* doing. There's no one else on this planet who knows about that except you."

David turns towards the visitors. "I'm sorry for this. We have parishioners who face challenges in life and seek our help when they are in this agitated state. We are not here to judge, but here to serve and help in the name of God." He points his hand in my direction.

As the elderly couple inch away from me towards the door of the gift shop, they look at each other and shift uncomfortably, treating me like a crazed lunatic who has recently been released from the local mental health unit.

Having heard the commotion from outside, one of David's colleagues enters, followed by two others. They circle around me, trying to contain my outburst as other visitors to the church arrive and hover in the doorway either out of curiosity or a keenness to help.

"Please," one lady says. In her sixties, with a kind face

and greying hair, she clasps her hands together as if praying as she attempts to calm me. "This is a place of God, not a place for acts of aggression. Whatever your concerns, we can talk about them in a civilised way. Perhaps you'd like to follow me outside so we can see how to help you."

"I don't need help. I want David to come clean about stalking me and sending anonymous messages to my place of business." I point a finger in David's direction. All I see now is red mist as my body shakes.

David shrugs his shoulders and rolls his eyes as if to suggest that I've lost the plot. "It can take a lot for a troubled soul to accept that they need support. Angry words, tears, and frustration are all cries for help."

A few people around David purse their lips, clasp their hands in anxious balls, and nod in agreement with compassionate smiles as they look at me. Can they not see how David is manipulating the situation against me? "No! I pound my fist into the palm of my hand. You don't know this man like I do. This is all a big game for him. Can't you see what he's trying to do here? He's trying to turn all of you against me. I'm not the bad person here."

My words fall on deaf ears as they continue staring at me.

"I'm sorry, but you are upsetting our parishioners, visitors, and members of staff. With kindness, I really must ask you to leave to avoid any further disruptions or we'll have to call the police."

As the woman's words turn frigid, my ex-husband's performance remains masterful, a villain cloaked in the guise of a saint. He stands before me, shoulders shrugged, eyes rolling with feigned innocence. Swayed by his charade, people around us offer me looks of pity and judgment, their compassion manipulated into a weapon against me. This is all a game to David, a twisted manipulation, landing the final blow in his gaslighting campaign. And there, amidst the murmurs of agreement, David's smirk unveils the true depth of his malevolence, a chilling reminder of the darkness lurking beneath his sanctimonious facade.

My face flushes in disbelief. If anything, I'm making my situation worse as my eyes moisten. Feeling defeated, I turn and rush out of the shop as everyone around me steps back and clears a path for my hasty exit. The sound of my feet tapping on the stone floor echoes around me as I push through the doors of the church and out into the fresh air. I collapse against the wall, my breath exhaling in ragged gasps as my head spins.

What just happened there?

18

MY BODY TINGLES as I shiver and shake. The adrenaline coursing through my system spikes my senses as I check my surroundings. Thankfully, there's no one around, and those in the church haven't followed me out, but my mind is awash with uncertainty and untamed anger. I haven't felt like this for years and the assault on my system leaves me dazed and confused. I hoped I had put these episodes in my past, but they are now coming at me thick and fast with alarming repetition.

There's a bench close by and holding on to the wall, I stagger towards it. I blink hard and try to focus, but I can already feel a thin film of sweat on my face as my cheeks redden. Panic swells in my chest as my vision fades in and out. I slump on to the bench and lean forward, pushing my head between my legs and taking long, deep, steady breaths to calm the raging inferno within me.

Bastard.

I can't be certain, but I know he's behind all of this. Day by day, he's been turning the screw on manipulating my life, making me doubt my thoughts and letting me unravel. Everything I've done to make myself whole again is crumbling around me, and I don't know what to do about it. My mind dances from one thought to another unable to grip any of them with certainty. I feel helpless and adrift, uncertain who to reach out to.

As my breathing steadies, I sit up and tip my head back towards the sky. Puffs of white clouds float by. They glide in the atmosphere, pure and untainted by anything that's happening down here. I wish I could be up there without a care in the world, gliding on the thermals like a flock of birds I can see in the distance.

I spot a pub across the road and get to my feet. It's not like me to drink during the day but I need one more than ever as I dart between the cars and push through its doors. It hasn't been open long and with only a few customers I feel like a deranged and desperate alcoholic needing their fix to steady their nerves and get them through the day. I'm not one of those, but after what I experienced, I still lean against the worn mahogany surface and order a double gin and tonic. The bartender takes my order but I can tell by her look she's questioning my choice of drink so early in the day.

Picking a corner table away from everyone, I settle down in the chair and cradle a drink between my hands before taking a sip and savouring the cool and refreshing taste on my lips. To be truthful, I rarely drink gin and tonic, and it doesn't taste like an alcoholic drink as I take an almighty gulp to quench the proverbial fire burning within me. The ice cubes clink the glass as I swirl the drink around in my hand before draining the rest and heading over to the bar to order another.

Again, the lady gives me a funny look but I'm beyond caring now. I need to numb the pain I feel inside. Taking my seat again, I grip my glass tight as I think about the anonymous email and how it's dredged up agonising memories of what David forced me to do during our marriage. It's why the picture of Freddie cut so deep. Amidst a fading world, one memory stands out—David's rape. It wasn't long after that I realised I was pregnant. I agonised over the discovery for weeks. Every part of my being wanted a child, but I was fraught with worry about the life I was bringing my baby into.

It took every ounce of courage to tell David about the pregnancy, and I can still see the visceral disgust on David's face even to this day upon hearing the news. I felt conflicted between moments of joy and deep sadness. That is why I am certain that it must be David who emailed me because only he would know about the loss and grief I will carry forever. I don't have proof, but no one else could craft the perfect words to inflict the deepest pain.

After I told him the news, I didn't have time to process his reaction since the subject wasn't up for discussion. He stormed out and left me alone most of the night before returning early in the morning and taking me against my will in bed as a punishment for my carelessness. The memory of his alcohol-laden breath lingers as he restrained me by my wrists, my desperate pleas for him to stop drowned out by his swearing, grunts, and moans.

Within forty-eight hours of that night, I was in a clinic having a termination. I cried through all of it, telling the nurse and doctor that my pregnancy was a mistake, even though I knew David had ignored all my pleas to discuss other options.

Salty tears collect on my lips as I stare into the bottom of my glass. I can't recall when I finish my second drink. There is nothing but melting ice now. Every day since that fateful one, I've grieved over the loss of my child. My precious baby.

As I think back to the picture of Freddie, I wonder if David only didn't want kids with me. Was I that much of a terrible choice in his eyes that he couldn't stand the thought of having a child with me? A chance to begin our family?

I rise to my feet swaying and go to order another double before returning. My head feels woozy, and my body isn't as tense.

That David now has a son with another woman only twists that knife deeper. He may not have harmed me with that revelation, but the news is enough to cause so much physical pain that I could lie on the floor and curl up into a ball praying for the pain to subside.

I pull my phone out of my bag and see that I've had two missed calls from Clive and three from Georgia. I know they worry about me, but at this moment it's the least of my concerns. In my hazy state, I type out a reply to them both, telling them I'm fine but need some space, so I won't be back in the office for the rest of the day.

As I toss the phone on to the table and sip my drink, I wonder if I can take much more.

19

A FEW WEEKS have passed with no further incidents. No dodgy emails. No random sightings of David. No visits to my neighbours. My HR manager, Kathy, has shown constant kindness by regularly checking in with me, yet she has taken no further action. And I appreciate her concern.

At first, I thought David lost interest in his game of cat and mouse, but now I'm more inclined to think that he's taken his family with him to start that new job in Surrey. Though not relieved, I feel I can start rebuilding the shattered pieces of my broken life. The last few months have been nothing but hell, and it's taken every ounce of willpower to get through every day. Anita hasn't been able to visit because of work commitments, but she keeps in touch by calling me a few times a week to make sure I'm okay and I've told her everything including the cryptic email, my conversation with Kathy, and how I confronted David in church. Though I'm happy every time I hear her voice, I'm always left with sadness that she's not here. I miss the impromptu coffee dates and catch-ups.

Mark has been my rock too. Even with his hectic schedule and occasional need to work away from home, he has lived up to his promise of being with me during every free moment that he has had. And tonight is no exception. He is treating me to a meal at Pizza Express in town. It's a place we've been many times. The food is good; the atmosphere buzzy, and it's a place where we can always relax.

We order dough balls and garlic butter to begin with. And once they arrive, we devour them.

I know Mark is busy at work, so I'm keen to find out what his plans are for the next few weeks. "When is this current contract finishing?"

Mark wipes his mouth and takes a sip from his Peroni beer. "I reckon we've got a week to go. Unfortunately, our next contract is over in Bury St Edmunds. We've had the electrical works subbed out to us on an office refurb. It might mean I have to stay over a few nights a week to work late as we're on a tight schedule."

"Oh." I look down at my drink and sigh, not enjoying the sinking feeling inside.

He reaches across and holds my hand. "Hey, listen. It will only be two or three weeks max. And I'll come back as much as I can. I might have to do a few weekends; I don't know. But the more hours we put in, the quicker the job gets done. You understand, don't you?"

I nod. It's wrong of me to expect him to give up his work for me, but I can't help feeling selfish. But perhaps things will be okay now. "I'm sure I'll be fine."

We brush our conversation to one side as the pizzas arrive. I enjoy each mouthful and there's little conversation between us as we both tuck in. It's only been in the last few weeks that I've got my appetite back. All the stress and anxiety over David didn't do wonders for my appetite

The Ex-Husband 127

or my weight, and the last time I weighed myself a few weeks ago I had lost six pounds through worry.

The restaurant is busy, and I soak up the warm atmosphere. There is a sea of smiling faces around me and it's so nice to feel normal. Just as I'm about to fork the last piece of pizza into my mouth, I pause. Standing on the pavement, I spot someone peering in. For a moment, I think it's David. I drop my fork, causing other diners to look. Mark stops and shoots me a look of concern before looking over his shoulder to follow my line of sight.

My heart is in my mouth as I take a second look. My stomach clenches in spasms before I let out a sigh of relief. It isn't David but someone who looks like him, but it's enough to send a spike of fear through me again.

"Are you okay, babes?" He shoots another glance over his shoulder before looking at me.

I clear my throat. "Ah... um... yes. Sorry. I thought I recognised someone."

Mark knows exactly who I mean as he reaches across and squeezes my hand. "He's gone now. I know it's difficult for you to come to terms with, but you've been so jittery ever since he appeared. And I'm worried about you and us."

"I'm fine, honestly." I brush off his concern and smile. "We're good. And I wouldn't be here now if it wasn't for you."

Mark smiles but the intention doesn't reach his face. He leans into the table and lowers his voice. "Jane, I know you're not fine. You can tell everyone that, but I know you better than all of them. I know this is still troubling you."

Sighing, I close my eyes for a second before opening them and looking at Mark. "He's gone and I'm relieved. I need to put it behind me and focus on us. I'm still the same old me."

Mark rests his elbows on the table and forms a steeple with his fingers. "If you're fine now and have put it behind you, why do you still keep checking all the doors and locks many times over every night? Why are you still peeking through the curtains every evening and looking for any sign of movement in the street or the back garden?"

What do I say? I hate keeping secrets from him. The last thing I want is for Mark to get hurt if David came after both of us. I can't tell him I still have recurring nightmares, seeing David's face above mine as he hurts me. I can't tell him I'm struggling at work because I'm having difficulty focusing. He would think I was being paranoid if I told him how I stop walking every few hundred yards to glance over my shoulder to see if anyone is following me. Just repeating it in my mind makes me sound crazy. What would Mark think?

I blow him a kiss. "I promise, everything is fine. It takes time to come to terms with what has happened. I buried all those painful memories with David. With him turning up, they all bubbled up to the top again. It takes time to push them back down again. That's all."

Mark tilts his head to one side. "You sure? You know you can tell me anything. I don't want you to hide anything from me. We're together and we need to support each other through good and bad times. So if there's anything on your mind please don't keep it to yourself. Promise?"

I smile. He's brilliant and I can't blame him for trying. He gets a medal for putting up with me and my crap. How can I be angry at that?

"I promise. How about we skip dessert and get the bill? We can go home and have our own sweet treat?" I know

The Ex-Husband 129

it's what we need as the stress of the last few weeks has taken a toll on our intimacy.

Mark sits back in his chair, wide-eyed at the suggestion. "Are you sure?"

"I won't be if you ask me again!" I narrow my eyes in mock frustration.

Mark raises his hand to catch a waiter's attention and we dash out minutes later and head back to mine.

20

I ROLL over in bed and stretch my arm out across to where Mark was lying. It still feels warm, and his pillow carries his scent as I nuzzle my face into it. Mark left early to get electrical supplies but not before wrapping his arms around me and holding me tight while planting soft kisses on my shoulder. He should be back, as he promised to have breakfast with me. I'm in a hazy state of wakefulness as I open my eyes and lie here for a few minutes.

Last night couldn't have finished better after the meal. We came back here and tore our clothes off in desperation as our mouths explored each other. By the time we made it to the upstairs landing we were already naked. Our lovemaking was intense, filled with hunger, want, and the need to be satisfied. I've rarely felt like that apart from in the early days of my marriage. But being married to David soon extinguished my desire for passion, love, and affection. Those things became taboo and things I grew to dread. David cast those to one side and replaced them with brutality, control, and punishment.

When I first got together with Mark, our lovemaking

was difficult. It was hard to let myself go because in my marriage I was often naked and frozen rigid with fear. Mark has been understanding and patient from the beginning. With time, my body learnt to relax, replacing fear with enjoyment. And last night was something I thought I wouldn't experience for a long time and perhaps ever.

A small smile forms on my face as I reminisce about Mark's expression of surprise when I became more adventurous in our relationship.

I throw the covers back and pad naked across the carpet into the hallway and to the bathroom, where I turn the dial on the shower, and wait for the water to warm up as I brush my teeth. My reflection in the mirror disappears behind a wall of steam. Stepping into the shower, I close my eyes and welcome the powerful jets as they pummel my back. I could stay in here for hours. There's something so relaxing about being in a shower, but the water company carved up our pavements and installed water metres in our street last year, so I'm mindful of how much the indulgence costs me.

I have to curtail my moment of happiness as I step out of the shower and dry myself off before slipping on my dressing gown and going back to my room to find something to wear. I rummage through my wardrobe, pushing hangers around until I settle on a white blouse, cream trousers, and black court shoes. Smart but functional I think as I check myself out in the mirror before heading downstairs to prepare breakfast.

It looks like the postman has arrived early today as I find a white envelope sitting on my doormat in the hallway. Reaching for it, I turn it over and feel confused. There's no name or address on it. Perhaps it's one of those generic envelopes containing a flyer from a char-

The Ex-Husband 133

ity, block paving driveway specialist, or gardening company, often dropped into every household. I take it with me as I head into the kitchen and drop it on the table before filling up the kettle and flicking on the switch.

As I wait for the kettle to boil, I turn and grab the envelope again and open it. Peering inside there are several pieces of paper which, when I unfold, leave my hands shaking. My heart thunders in my chest and I stagger back having to grab a chair for support. Blinking hard, I can't take in what I'm seeing. Am I dreaming? I drop the sheets on the table in a hurry as if they're too hot to handle before I sit down and stare at them in disbelief. An overwhelming sense of dread washes over me. Just as I thought I had put it all behind me in recent weeks, it's started again.

I can't bear to bring myself to glance at the images any longer, instead concentrating on the kitchen cupboard on the wall opposite to me. But I know I need to look. I need to be sure.

Closing my eyes briefly and preparing myself, I open them to stare at the images. They are pictures of me in and around town. Someone has been following me. But it gets worse than that. Somehow, the images have been edited to look like I'm in an embrace with a man and he's kissing me. And it's not Mark. More to the point, I don't know who that man is.

As I push the images to one side, the last sheet of paper reveals a chilling threat.

Wait until Mark sees these!

This can't be happening. As I jump from my seat and race to the lounge window and throw back the net curtain, I scan the street for anyone hanging around who looks out of place. But the street is empty.

There's only one person who could do this. David. But he's been quiet for weeks, so I assume he's moved to Surrey. But it wouldn't stop him from driving over and posting this through my letter box.

I clutch my arms around my chest as I pace the lounge trying to make sense of this, but I'm shaken from my thoughts as the doorbell rings. Mark is at the door and at once spots my state of distress as I have my teeth clamped around my bottom lip.

He comes in and places his hands on my arms, studying my face with concern. "What happened? Are you okay?"

I blow out my cheeks and go to the kitchen before returning with the images. "I found these in an envelope on my doorstep when I came down." He takes them from me and studies them for a few moments, before looking up at me, his face a mixture of concern and surprise.

"What are these?" He waves them in front of me. "Who's the bloke?" He pulls his shoulders back and stares at me.

"I don't know who he is. Someone has been following me around and taking pictures of me. They've doctored the photos to look as if I'm with someone. It must be David."

Mark brings the images closer so he can study them. "Doctored? They look legit to me."

I shrug. "I'm not sure how you doctor images, but someone definitely has. David could be the one, but I can't be certain. He was a computer science lecturer, and now works in IT. He knows how to use Photoshop. Whoever it was has done this to create the impression that I'm cheating on you. That last sheet implies they were

The Ex-Husband 135

going to tell you. Since I have nothing to hide, I'm telling you first." As I move closer to Mark, we are now inches away from each other. With a gentle touch, I place my hand on his cheek and gaze into his eyes. I can see the pain and confusion behind them. "I promise you, nothing is going on. There is no other man. I wouldn't do this to you. It's not me. If I had something to hide I wouldn't be telling you, let alone showing you this, would I?"

It takes a moment before Mark nods. "What are you going to do about this?"

"I'm going to find out if any of the neighbours noticed anyone coming to my door. Whoever it was came here after you left, and you've only been gone ninety minutes. And then I'm going to the police."

"Do you want me to come with you?"

I appreciate Mark's offer, but I know I have to do this myself. "No, babe. You go to work. I'm going to phone in sick and speak to my HR manager. Once I've been to the police, I'll call you with an update. Okay?"

"As long as you are sure?"

"Absolutely sure. I need this to stop. If it's David, then I need to get him off our backs, even if it means involving the police."

NEEDING TO DOWNPLAY MY CONCERNS, I go door to door and ask my neighbours if they spotted any delivery drivers or leaflet droppers going from house to house.

Chrissy has seen nobody, and nothing has dropped through her letter box, so my suspicions are getting stronger. She asks lots of questions because that's what Chrissy does. Inquisitive and nosey. I bat off her concerns and come up with an excuse about a roofing flyer coming through my door but for whatever reason the contact details were missing as the leaflet had been smudged in printing. Chrissy, not being one to miss out on an opportunity offers to rummage through her drawers in the lounge for the number of a roofer that she has kept. I decline the offer and thank her before walking off, leaving the woman clinging on to her cardigan while she carries on talking.

A few of my neighbours aren't in, and the few that I do talk to have seen no one this morning. The lack of sightings doesn't help, but it confirms my suspicions that if it was David, he was clever at not being spotted.

I try one of the last few neighbours, Mrs Casey. She's a lovely lady. A widow with two grown-up children who have moved away. She always stops me in the street and shows me pictures of her grandchildren who she wishes she spent more time with. But with her son in Cardiff and her daughter in Manchester, family get-togethers are few. Mrs Casey is warm and welcoming as she answers the door. She begs me to come in for a cup of tea and a natter, but I lie and tell her I'm late for work. My heart lurches as I see the disappointment on her face as her shoulders drop and the cheery smile turns into a frown.

"I'm sorry, but I promise to come over for a cuppa in the next few days. Currently, I have a lot going on." I spin the same yarn I used on Chrissy but draw a blank. Now it's my turn for my shoulders to sag. As I'm about to turn, Mrs Casey's eyes light up.

"Oh, Jane. I don't know if he was a roofer, but I saw someone about an hour ago." She raises her hand to her lips as she narrows her eyes in thought. "Or perhaps longer than that. I can't be sure."

I'm all ears as I take a step closer to her door. "Did you get a good look at them?"

The Ex-Husband

Mrs Casey grimaces. "Not really, love. I noticed someone heading back down the road. They had a big coat on, hood up, and they were looking down at the ground. Walking quickly, to be fair. As if in a hurry."

"Tall? Short? White? Black? Asian?"

Mrs Casey purses her lips and shakes her head. "Sorry. They had their back to me when I saw them. If it had been a few moments earlier, I would have had a better look at their face."

I sigh in resignation as the frustration gnaws away at my thoughts. "Okay, thanks, anyway. I better get back. I'll speak to you soon."

As I trudge back to my house, I'm none the wiser. I have no choice now but to go to the police.

21

POLICE STATIONS ALWAYS FEEL ODD. They're supposed to be a place of safety, but why does it feel like I've done something wrong? The walls have a bland cream colour, and they screw down the plastic chairs to the floor. It's a less than welcoming place as I stare at the noticeboard to my left. There are various posters about crime prevention and helpline numbers. My eyes home in on a particular poster offering suggestions to women who walk home at night alone. *What about women who walk alone during the day?*

There's another woman sitting on a chair at the other end of the waiting area. She pushes back and forth a pram with a sleeping toddler. There are remnants of orange crisp crumbs around the little boy's face and then the evidence of what caused it, a pack of cheesy wotsits stuffed down by the side of his leg. The mother looks like she's lost in her own world as she stares transfixed at the wall opposite us. I wonder what she's here for?

The male civilian officer behind the counter tilts his head forward and looks over the top of his glasses at both of us but offers no apology for the wait. I have been sitting here for twenty-five minutes, and it seems like they are still trying to find an officer for me. It's a bloody police station for crying out loud.

It seems like the mum is as fed up as she pipes up. "Is it going to be long?" she spits as she glares at him. "My boy is going to wake up soon and before you know it, he'll scream the place down."

"Not long," is the reply as the officer glares at the woman for a few seconds before he carries on with his paperwork at the desk. For all I know he's doing a crossword and doesn't appreciate being disturbed as I clock him throwing a little shake of his head.

Outside, I hear the frenzy of police sirens and then see flashing blue lights as two police cars whizz past the main door in a blur. Seconds later, another police car and van fly past no doubt attending the same shout. Does that mean there are even fewer officers now to see us? I let out a sigh and wonder what my life has come to. I've never needed to call on the help of the police. Everything was going so well until a few months ago. Now it feels like my life is in a tailspin and out of control. It takes every ounce of courage to step out of my house. I'm forever peeking through my curtains like a nosey neighbour, looking for any signs of trouble. Any signs of David. I can't walk the streets of Cambridge city centre without my eyes scanning the crowds. I am perpetually in a heightened state of alert, and it hasn't been beneficial for my health either. Constant tension headaches have plagued me, and I spend the whole day feeling like there's a ball of anxiety doing somersaults inside my belly.

Will it ever end? Can I ever get my life back?

"Jane Trebble?" A voice makes me jump. I look up to notice a young lady by the double doors to my left. She's not what I expect. Dressed in a pair of jeans and T-shirt with her ID card on a lanyard draped around her neck. She looks in her early twenties with long dark hair pulled into a high ponytail.

"Um... Yes..." I jump to my feet.

"Hello there, I'm Detective Constable Jess Carter." She smiles as she lifts her ID badge towards me. "Would you like to come with me?"

I nod, not knowing what else to say. I follow her as she swipes her card by the double doors and then takes me along a corridor and into a small interview room. It has two comfy chairs and a small round table between them. There's nothing on the walls, not even a photo frame. I assume they refrain from decorating the walls to prevent them from being used as a weapon to attack an officer. Whatever the reason, the room is dull and lifeless, with grey-coloured walls and a dark grey carpet.

"Please, take a seat." Detective Carter closes the door behind us. I take the seat closer to the window.

Once we're both seated, DC Jess Carter opens her notepad and looks across at me with a warm and reassuring smile. "I understand from the officer on the front desk that you are being harassed and stalked? Would you like to tell me more?"

I wonder where to begin. The best way to start is with the doctored photos from this morning. I pull them out of my bag and pass them on to her. "These came in an envelope this morning. Someone had posted them through my letter box." I lay the sheets of paper on the table between us. "Someone has been following me and taking pictures of me. They then doctored the images to make it look like I'm giving this person a kiss."

The detective looks through the different images. "Do you know the person in them?"

"No. Your guess is as good as mine, as I don't know

who it is. I'm in a relationship, and I showed these images to my boyfriend Mark this morning. Somehow my stalker has taken photographs of me and... I guess... superimposed them with whoever this person is." I jab a finger at the images.

The detective reads the message about telling Mark. She makes a note of what I've said. "And there was something about emails you received at work?"

"Yes." I retrieve copies from my bag and hand them over to her.

The DC nods again and adds to her notes. "Has anyone been giving you unwanted attention at work, regardless of whether they are male or female? Or has there been any office flirting?"

"No. I get on with everyone at work. They're all lovely."

"Do you socialise with many of your work colleagues outside of work?"

My mind goes back to the meals and drinks I've shared with Georgia, Clive, Abnash, Annette, Lucy, and Priya. I can't imagine any of them doing anything like this. They don't have a bad bone in their bodies. "I do," I reply and spring to their defence as if they've done something wrong. "But we get on well and I've never fallen out with any of my friends."

I tell the detective constable about my documents disappearing from my computer and the IT servers, and how Kiran in IT support couldn't find them.

"You told our front desk officer about harassment. Who do you suspect is harassing you?"

I tilt my head back and let out a sigh. "My ex-husband David Marchant. A few months ago I spotted him in the city centre and these things have been happening since he arrived."

"What leads you to believe that it's him?"

The Ex-Husband

I have no idea where to begin, and I question whether she will trust anything I say. "I was married to David for several years. It was a very difficult marriage. He was abusive, violent, and controlling. With the help of my friend Anita, I escaped Norfolk, I divorced him, and moved to Cambridge to start a new life. I wanted to get away from him."

"Did you report him at the time?"

Lowering my head, I shake it in disbelief. "I was too scared to call the police." I doubted whether they would believe me. The thought of being in court and having to describe how he beat me, raped me, stopped me from seeing my friends, and controlled everything I ate, wore, or did was unbearable. I already felt humiliated, embarrassed, and angry with myself. When you're in that situation, there's a part of you that accept it rather than attract further attention to yourself. I wasn't strong enough to deal with it, or see my life played out in court."

The detective constable smiles and gives me time to compose myself when she notices my hands shaking. "Are you okay? Can I get you a glass of water?"

I nod.

She leaves the room and comes back a few minutes later with two glasses of water, and hands me one. I thank her and take a sip, welcoming the liquid as it moistens my parched mouth.

"And you believe he is behind these events?"

I shrug. "I can't think of anyone else."

"How does it explain the missing files and documents at work? Does David work in your organisation?"

I haven't got an answer to that question. I'm mystified. Perhaps it was a freak error, a coincidence, or a mistake that I made.

"And you believe he tracked you down and started a campaign of harassment?"

"Who else can it be? David could have ended up in any other town or city in the UK. What are the chances of him ending up in Cambridge and living a few minutes away from me?" I tell her about David's family and the photograph of his son, and how by chance his partner, Siobhan, also lives in Cambridge.

"So it could be a coincidence?" DC Carter asks, as she looks up from her notes.

I lean forward and run a hand through my hair. My eyes are tired and my body aches. As each minute passes it becomes harder to think. "I don't know what to believe now. All I know is that I moved to Cambridge and started a new life with a great job and wonderful partner. And everything was working out well... until he arrived. I seem to bump into him everywhere I go. Whenever I'm in town, he is there. He even knows where I live because I saw him *allegedly* dropping leaflets from the church along my street. I'm scared because I know what he's capable of."

"I appreciate your concerns. And we take harassment and stalking seriously. What kind of threatening language or behaviour has he used since he turned up?"

This is where my whole case collapses. As soon as I open my mouth and reply, my argument for accusing him will seem flimsy, as he has done nothing illegal. "He hasn't used abusive language, or intimidated me, or been aggressive. He's careful to keep his threats veiled."

The detective looks up from her notes again and studies me. I can see the hopelessness in her eyes. She's got nothing to go on.

I hold up my hand in defence before she can reply. "I know how it sounds. Trust me, if I were in your position, I understand it would sound absurd to me. He's very

The Ex-Husband 145

manipulative and charming. When we lived together he was the model citizen outside of our home. People loved him. They gushed about him. Despite being well regarded in academia, he was a monster behind closed doors. He would lock the front and back doors so I couldn't leave unless he was with me. He took away my mobile phone and only let me answer it when he was standing there." There is so much more I could tell her, but I wonder how much of it she would take seriously. I haven't even told her about the abortion or the punishment beatings in the kitchen and bedroom yet.

"So how did he treat you when you met him in the street?"

"Like everyone else he meets. He is very pleasant. A measured tone. He doesn't raise his voice and keeps his distance. To anyone passing by, he would seem harmless."

The detective puts her notes down and locks her fingers together before resting them on her lap. "Because he hasn't threatened you verbally or physically, it makes it harder for us to bring him in for questioning. Do you have an address for him?"

The second she says that I realise how little I know about his new life, and how much he knows about mine. "No. But I know he works at the church on Hills Road. He helps in the gift shop and the mobile soup kitchen for the homeless. I'm sorry, that's all I know."

"Okay, Jane, leave it with me. I'll discuss this with my sergeant, and we'll pay him a visit to find out what he's up to." She hands me her business card. "Here are my contact details. I'm glad you raised it with us, and if there are any other further incidents in and around your home or at work, then please do give me a call. I would advise you to make sure where possible that you're with someone at home or outdoors, and don't walk home alone at night.

Also, make sure you're keeping detailed notes about these incidents. Dates. Times. Everything."

I thank her as she shows me out and walks me to my car parked in a visitors' bay. As I sit behind my wheel, I'm uncertain what my visit achieved. Yes, I've logged my concerns, and they are now on the system, but I grapple with the fact the law can't protect me from David unless he slips up. I thump the steering wheel in frustration. I'm sick of feeling so scared, and I realise I'll have to outsmart him if I'm to reclaim my life once more.

In the end, my salvation rests in my own hands.

22

I EDGE through the traffic as I make my way home. My mind feels so confused, and I'm not sure which way to turn next. It feels like everything is becoming too much for me. For the past few months, my life has been nothing but a whirlwind of emotions. Just as I feel there is an end in sight, something else trips me up and send me back into a dark place I thought I had left behind many years ago. Yet, amidst the chaos, a tiny spark of defiance flickers within me, a silent vow that I won't let my past define my future.

David has always been a manipulator. Thinking back on it now, it was there right from the start, but I never noticed it. The red flags were waving, but bundled up inside my love bubble, I ignored them. Simple things like walking round Sainsbury's. I would pick up one item and he would shake his head, disagreeing with my choice, so I would end up replacing it on the shelf as he chose something else instead.

If we were going out for date night and I selected my outfit, he would take something else out of the wardrobe for me to wear and tell me I looked even more gorgeous if I wore his choice. At the time I believed it was mere flattery and I would accept his choice, thinking he would love me even more.

But I guess such behaviour was his way of beginning to flex his control over me. I was too in love to notice it and pleased that my husband took such an interest in my life. How stupid I was.

If I explained the beginnings of my marriage to anyone now, it would be clear to them and me that David valued control more than anything. Despite being subtle, the man *always* got his way. Even with sex, if I wanted to go on top, he would refuse saying he preferred to be on top.

I slow in traffic and wait at the red lights. I sigh as I look at people walking past. A woman in her late thirties or early forties waddles past carrying two heavy bags of shopping. Her face is strained, and I can see the handles stretching. I wonder how long it'll be before they give way and her shopping spills out across the street. I would feel sorry for her, but I can imagine how funny it would be to see her groceries spill out over the pavement and her frantic attempts to gather them together.

My attention turns towards a few lads of school age congregating under the bus shelter. They all stare into their phones, no conversation between them. I wonder if they even know how to have a civilised conversation these days. They're living out their lives through tech and social media.

The lights turn green, I pull off again and return my thoughts to my life and to him. He controlled and dominated every aspect of my life and as each year passed, he tightened the screw, stripping my soul and my identity. Bit by bit he wore me down, turning from Mr Nice to Mr

Nasty until I became a recluse at home. It was up to him when I could leave the house, who I spoke to, what I wore, and even what I ate. He would watch me from the doorway as I went to throw the kitchen rubbish bag into the bin outside.

If I was out there when my neighbours, Nisha or Sunil, were throwing out their rubbish, David would glare at me if I stopped to be neighbourly towards them. At first, he would punish me by giving me the cold shoulder for a few hours. Then it escalated to him shouting at me when his lunch or dinner was not to his exacting standards, before becoming physical, where he would grab me by my throat the minute I came back in and pin me against the wall, his hot breath pounding my face as he snarled at me.

It's hard to explain what it's like to have the freedom taken away from your life. David even took away my bank card and would give me thirty pounds in cash every week, and from that I would have to buy all the food, toiletries, and household cleaning products. No wonder he would beat the shit out of me when all I could give him were simple meals.

"I give you all this money and is this all you can provide me?" he would hiss and push his plate away. I tried to avoid setting off David's explosive rages. He was so unpredictable, he terrified me.

"Get up, you lazy bitch!" That was all I heard when he woke me in the middle of one night and made me have a cold shower before forcing himself on me on the bathroom floor. Then there were the times he demanded that I leave the bathroom door unlocked so he had the option to walk in on me as I didn't deserve any privacy. The memories tighten my chest as tears flood my vision.

You learn quickly not to raise your voice and to hide your bruises under baggy long-sleeved tops and scarves.

Any sign of resistance, non-compliance, or defiance were a direct challenge to his authority.

It was only because of Anita that I found the strength to escape from David's grasp and once I was away from him, I pushed for divorce. It's the reason David hates her so much. Anita threw me a lifeline and stood up to him in much the same way she did on her recent visit. And without her here, the sense of vulnerability has once again crept back into my life.

The streets pass me in a blur as I head towards my house. Though I'm free of my toxic relationship and marriage, I know deep down I'm still haunted by the damage David caused me, and I still carry the mental and physical scars.

23

It's taken me ninety minutes to reach Norfolk and find Anita's address. Plenty of time for me to be alone with my thoughts and what I'll do. She's been troublesome from the start and I can't afford to let her ruin my plans. I think I've done a pretty job of gaslighting Jane. I explained how we weren't suited to each other as a married couple because of *her* issues and the interference of others. I've sown the seed of self-doubt to get past her bullshit antenna. I've told her many times that I only wish to be friends and to clear the air before I leave because I'm not interested in her.

But I'm not leaving without her. Jane got away from me. She slipped through my fingers, and I want her back. It took time and dedication to break her down and make her compliant. All the courting, showering her with gifts, and confessing my undying love for her served as a precursor to winning her over and taking control of her life. She's mine. I'm not letting that effort go to waste.

However, Anita still poses a threat to my plans. With

her around, Jane has support and the will to challenge me.

That can't happen.

It feels strange being back here again. A melancholy interlude as memories flood my awareness. I think of many happy moments that have left their mark on my life, then I grip the steering wheel as I'm reminded of the not so pleasant memories and the reason I am here.

Anita... Dear Anita. She was a thorn in my side and the one who undid all my good work. She's the reason Jane escaped, and now she'll face the consequences for meddling in my life.

I've chosen the cover of night for my arrival and the ability to move unseen when fewer eyes are around. It made sense for me to move under the shadow of darkness. With my lights off, and my car parked in a turning opposite her house, I need to wait for her return. If I've timed it correctly, she should arrive in the next twenty minutes. Her routine appears to be the same every weekday night from what I've observed. She arrives home about seven-thirty p.m., pours a glass of wine and heads upstairs to fill the bath.

With plenty of time to spare I step from my car, a bath towel in hand, and close the door before crossing the road and sticking to the shadows as I approach her house. The coast is clear. I slip down the side of the property, opening the wooden gate that leads to her small garden. The riskiest part is over as I am shielded from her neighbours by tall hedges and bushes that she lets grow wild and natural.

Pulling a large-bladed screwdriver from inside my jacket, I wedge the tip in the window and push hard until the mechanism breaks free allowing me to climb in and land inside her kitchen. I know she lives alone, but I stay

The Ex-Husband

still for a few seconds and listen for any noise before closing the window.

I spend the next few minutes wandering around in the darkness going from room to room. I'd happily set this place alight because every room I enter reminds me of her. Everything is loud and bold, just like her mouth. My fists curl into balls as I hover in the hallway. I need to find somewhere to hide, and having opened a few doors, I settle for the space beneath the stairs as it's the only door without a lock.

Though it's cramped and stuffy, I wait and before I know it, I hear the keys in the front door and the whoosh as it drags on the carpet. Footsteps pad past me and into the kitchen as the keys clatter on the worktop. She hums a tune as she busies herself with preparing her meal and I hear the chink of a glass... wine.

It's a few minutes before the microwave chimes and the door open and close. Like clockwork. And it's seconds later that she pads past me again and heads upstairs. *Wait,* I tell myself as the impatience grows within me.

From somewhere within the house I hear the flexing of copper pipes as water gushes through them. It seems an eternity to fill the bath, and when silence returns, I push the door open and check to make sure the coast is clear. She's turned the hallway lights on, and the pelmet lights beneath the kitchen cupboards light up the worktops. From where I stand, I see a bottle of wine on the worktop, condensation forming on the outside. As I head towards the bottom of the stairs, I remove my shoes to prevent leaving marks on the carpet and clench my teeth in frustration while she persists in humming and singing. The sound of splashing water creeps through the open bathroom door as I take each step making sure my steps are light and the stairs don't creak.

With Anita oblivious to my presence, I peer through the open gap in the door and see the back of her head resting above the top of the bath. I take a further few minutes to edge the door open a few centimetres at a time until it's wide enough for me to slip through. Now I'm a few feet behind her as I place my bath towel on the floor. I can see the top of her breasts resting among the foamy bath water. She is within touching distance as I creep forward holding my hands out ready to grab her.

I take one last, lingering look at the bitch. Her singing drowns out my movement, before I lunge forward and grab her hair, pushing her head beneath the water. Her hands thrash and grab at my arms but now the full weight of my body is bearing down on her as I push deeper. Muffled screams bubble up to the surface as her legs flail, sending sprays of water across the tiles and floor. She fights hard to push my arms away as her face bobs back above the water. Her hands frantically reach for the sides of the bath, so with one hand on top of her head and my other over her face, I pull her back and down again. Each gasp, plea, or moan only make me more determined at my task. I clench my jaw determined to make her death as terrifying as possible.

Her feet slam into the far end of the bath as her knees buckle, and her body sinks deeper into the water. Through a clearing in the bubbles, her terrified eyes gaze up at me, wide and in pain. Not long now. I keep the pressure, fighting the urge within myself to pull her out and break every bone in her body as I tear her limb from limb. Panicked gurgles fill the room before Anita's body goes limp and silent. I watch as her figure sinks deeper. Her eyes fixate on me, wide and empty, as if asking, "why?"

The fight has left me breathless as I stand up and stare at her lifeless form. I'll give her credit, she put up a fight, but the element of surprise caught her when she was most vulnerable.

Now for the hard part, staging it like she's the victim of a tragic accident. I pushed down on her head and not her body so there should be no visible bruising. And unless the pathologist shaves her head, the bruising to her scalp will be harder to find. I plunge my arms into the bathwater and slide my hands beneath her armpits so I can haul her a little out of the water. It takes all my strength to hold her body to one side as I drop it back down. Her head hits the bath with an almighty thud. I want to make it look like she slipped and hit her head on the bath before drowning. Evidence of water in her lungs will add weight to that premise, and the bruising to the side of the head will back it up.

I'm drenched now, but that's fine. After running my fingers through my hair and tidying myself up, I check the space round me to make sure I haven't left anything behind as I grab my bath towel and wipe my hands and arms. The towel, my clothes, and shoes will end up in various bins somewhere along my journey back to Cambridge. I'll change out of them once I'm away from here as I don't want to leave any hair or clothing fibres for the forensic services.

I take one last look at Anita's body, a satisfying grin spreading across my face.

24

"*How am I to go to work wearing this crumpled shirt?*" *David shouts as he charges out of the bedroom and thunders down the stairs to track me down in the kitchen.*

I'm washing up the breakfast dishes even though we have a dishwasher. David says it would be too easy for me if I kept using it, and for that reason he cut the plug off the lead. I look over my shoulder to see David standing in the doorway holding up his favourite pink shirt, which he always wears on Wednesday, so I iron it the day before. But today is Monday. Even though my hands are submerged in hot water, I feel an icy chill creeping through my body.

"Well?" His voice rises again as he closes the gap between us, his face now only inches away from me. As his cheeks redden, a lattice of red veins fills his eyes, revealing the hate in his expression.

"I'm sorry. It's just that you wear it on..." I don't have time to finish my sentence. His hand clamps round my throat and sends me hurtling back towards the dining table. I gasp for air as a searing heat spreads across my neck, my body arching, and my legs dangling off the floor.

"Pleeeease," I splutter, *"I'm sorry."*

"Sorry?!" he shouts. *"Sorry? That's not good enough. You pathetic woman. I've now got to iron my shirt myself. Do you honestly think I've got time for that?"* He snarls, his eyes fixed wide with pure hatred.

He lets go of my throat and grabs me by the hair, pulling me off the table and on to the floor. I'm on my hands and knees now being dragged across the kitchen floor as I grit my teeth. I know not to scream. David beat that into me a long time ago.

"When are you going to learn?" He sits on top of me, pinning me to the floor and raises a hand above his head. My eyes widen as terror grips me. I watch as his fingers curl into a fist seconds before it heads towards me.

"No!" I scream, thrusting my hand out to block it.

"Jane!" Mark shouts as he reaches for my arms. I'm thrashing in bed, my mind reliving those moments as if they're real. While Mark is lying asleep beside me, I've lashed out, my hand connecting with his face.

Focusing in the dark, I blink hard and see Mark sitting up in bed, his hand over his nose and mouth. "You punched me in the face."

"I'm sorry." I sit up and hide my face behind my hands as I cry. "I was having a nightmare."

Mark sniffs and wipes the moisture from his eyes. "No shit. Jesus, that hurt. It made my eyes water."

"I'm so sorry. I didn't mean to hurt you." Tears spill from my eyes.

Mark pulls me close and wraps his arm around me as we fall back on to the pillows. "Hey, it's okay."

"No, it's not okay. I hurt you. I know I haven't told you much about how David treated me and what he did to me, but I promise I will soon. My nightmare was about him attacking me in the kitchen one day. It was horrible. It felt so real, like it was happening all over again."

The Ex-Husband

"It's okay. You don't need to explain. I hate what he's done to you. God knows what I'll do if I ever meet him face to face." Mark strokes my hair. "He's the one we should be angry with. You've done nothing wrong."

I know everything Mark says makes sense, but my mind is a tangled mess, and deep down I'm fighting an internal battle that makes me think I'm losing the plot. I'm damaged goods. Why would Mark want to put up with that for the rest of his life? I'm not sure where to begin when I tell him. The repeated sexual assaults, the forced abortion, the stripping away of my identity which has left me questioning who am I? Is there much of the old me left?

Amidst the turmoil, a faint glimmer of hope flickers within me—I can sense the essence of who I once was, buried but not lost. It's a daunting journey ahead, but I'm resolved to rediscover my strength, to piece together the fragments of my former self.

As my heartbeat gradually returns to normal and my racing thoughts still, we lie in each other's arms for the next few hours, neither of us able to fall asleep again as daylight breaks through the curtains.

There's little said between us as we both rise and throw on dressing gowns before heading down to make some coffee. While I sit at the table, Mark makes the coffee in silence, adding a few slices of bread in the toaster for us. The tension still lingers between us, and I feel so upset for hurting Mark even though it wasn't deliberate.

25

WITH MY CURTAINS drawn and the door shut, I've converted my spare room into a monitoring station. A large office desk and a big thirty-six-inch curved screen afford me the luxury of checking the live feeds from the tiny cameras I've hidden in Jane's house. There is not much of her life that I won't be privy to as I connect to the application and four mini feeds appear on my monitor.

A bristle of excitement flutters through me, and I sense a shift in my breathing. I grab the mouse and roll the cursor across all four feeds. This is better than I imagined. Though each feed is in black and white, it doesn't take away from the fact that the images are clear. I'm amazed at how much technology they can squeeze into tiny, microscopic cameras these days.

All seems quiet to begin with. Jane and Mark are lying in bed and nothing seems to happen for a while. My groin twitches when I see Jane throw back the covers to reveal her naked body. She's always been slim for as long as I've known her, and she dresses well, but I'm sure many men imagine what she looks like naked and would pay good money to see what I can see now. I click on the bedroom monitor to increase the size of the screen so I can examine her in finer detail. Jane slides out from the bed and throws on her dressing gown before heading to the bathroom. Mark rises a few seconds after her and throws on his robe too before disappearing and reappearing a short while later in the kitchen.

I shrink that screen down and switch to the bathroom monitor feed. She closes the door and slips off her robe, hanging it on the bathroom door before sitting on the toilet to have a wee. This is incredible. I let out a laugh before throwing a hand over my mouth as if she might hear me down the feed. If she knew I was watching her every move, it would horrify her. She yawns and runs a hand through her messy hair before getting up and flushing the toilet, washing her hands and throwing her robe back on.

There is a momentary pause as I lose sight of her. She must be on the landing because she is not back in her bedroom. It's not long before she reappears in the kitchen, taking a seat at the table. I study the interaction between them. They're not saying much to each other. In fact, nothing. He's making them breakfast and she's staring at him. I need to review the footage from last night in case I missed something.

I sit here rocking back and forth in my chair while watching the screens. It's getting boring now. It must be how CCTV operators in control rooms feel. Probably nothing happens for a long time and their concentration wanes as does their interest.

It's another thirty minutes before Jane gets up and heads upstairs, leaving Mark to wash up. Let's hope it hots up as I sit up in my chair again and fix my attention on the screen as I watch Jane head back into the bathroom and

The Ex-Husband

163

hang her robe up on the back of the door. She turns on the shower and steps in. I can see her for a few moments before the room fills with steam and the lens from my camera clouds over. Ah, I hadn't thought of that. As much as I was looking forward to pleasuring myself while I watch Jane in the shower, I hadn't considered the steam factor. Schoolboy error.

Never mind, it felt like a good idea at the time. I'm treated to further glimpses of Jane's naked body not long after she dries herself and heads to her bedroom, slipping on a pair of knickers and a bra, before choosing clothes from her wardrobe.

Mark comes up and joins her in the bedroom, walking over to her and wrapping his arms around her. I wish I could hear what they were saying, because they kiss and it's not long before Mark slips his robe off and the two of them fall on to the bed for a quickie.

I grit my teeth and my left eye twitches as I watch. It should be me taking her. Not him. With her trousers around her ankles, he is taking her from behind. It's too much for me to bear as I switch off the monitor and throw my mouse against the wall. Bitch.

This was supposed to have been fun, but it's not. I don't want to see her having sex with her boyfriend when it should be me.

Pushing back in my chair, I tip my head back and stare at the closed blinds. It started off as a good idea and seeing Jane get out of bed naked was a highlight, but I'm not sure I can put myself through seeing her and Mark at it. One thing is definite, I can't wait to see her and meet her gaze without her even suspecting that I've been observing her.

The thought returns a smile to my face as I pull myself away from the screen and turn my attention to my next task of sending Jane a present. I take a large envelope from the drawer in my desk and stuff a pair of Jane's white knickers in it along with a typed message. No need to give her clues who I am with my handwriting. A strip of Sellotape seals the envelope to avoid leaving a saliva trace, and I'm ready to drop it off to her.

26

AFTER THE HORRID night and that dreadful nightmare, it felt as though things shifted between me and Mark. He was a little distant at breakfast and wanted answers about my life. He wanted to know more, but I couldn't give him more details. I didn't want us to start on a bad note and after my shower he came up to apologise. He was so sweet, and I don't know what came over us other than a desperate urge for us to reconnect, which we did.

With Mark off to work, I'm now more desperate than ever for the truth. I need to know for sure if David is the person responsible for some or all of the recent disruption in my life. My head tells me it is, but I need to prove it. I've not fallen out with anyone at work, nor have I with any of my neighbours, so it has to be him. David is very clever. He's pulled the wool over everyone's eyes in the past and they all thought that butter wouldn't melt in his mouth. Only I knew the truth behind the false sincerity and kindness he displayed to those we met.

Since crossing paths in Cambridge, I realise I know little about his life here other than his work at the church and his family, but it feels like he knows so much about my new life. And it's the family where I need to start. Call me crazy, and I'm feeling that way, but I need answers fast, even though I feel like my life is fraying at the seams.

With a renewed vigour in my step and before I can talk myself out of it, I grab my keys, jump in the car, and head to the Royal Papworth Hospital. As I make my way there, I'm not even sure where to begin or what to say. Do I go to reception and tell them I'm looking for Siobhan, a nurse?

I realise as I'm driving I don't have a surname for her. Are they married? I remember David saying he had a partner, Siobhan, and a little boy. Did the fact he labelled the woman his partner mean they're living as a couple but aren't married? I don't know. Shit. There could be a dozen Siobhans working at the hospital. Then what? My mind races.

I run through multiple scenarios as I follow the signs to Royal Papworth Hospital and it's not long before I head to the visitors' car park and make my way to reception. There's a small shop by the entrance. With quick thinking, and to make my visit more authentic, I pay for a box of chocolates. There are two people manning the front desk, both women, and I wait in line behind a small queue until it's my turn. All I can hear is, "I have an appointment for this and an appointment for that." I tap my foot as my impatience grows.

It's finally my turn as I step up to the counter and lean in towards Perspex glass. The receptionist doesn't greet me with a smile but looks up at me. "How can I help you?" Her voice is dull and monotone.

I fidget with the car keys in my hand while still thinking of what to say. She looks at me and raises a brow as if to say, "well get on with it."

The Ex-Husband 167

"I... wonder if you can help me. I'm looking for one of your nurses who helped a friend of mine before she passed away. She was so kind that I want to thank her in person for the care and attention she gave my friend before..." *Think of a name quick,* "Natasha passed away."

The receptionist narrows her eyes and views me with suspicion. "Do you have a name?"

"Nurse Siobhan. Sorry Tasha gave me her surname, but I've forgotten."

"A department?"

I don't know that either. God, I'm crap at lying. "Um... Tasha was in the respiratory disease ward and developed sepsis. They couldn't save her."

A thin line forms as the receptionist purses her lips. I wince knowing she's frustrated with me as she taps away on her keyboard. "We have five Siobhans here." She pauses for a second as she studies her screen, all the while throwing me a fleeting glance. Perhaps she senses my nerves as I smile back. A part of me wants to turn and bolt for the main doors. I'm not sure I can hold my nerve.

"Freddie!" I shout, almost making myself jump.

"Pardon?"

"Sorry, I remember Tasha saying that Nurse Siobhan had a three-year-old son called Freddie. She showed Tash a picture on her phone. Blonde boy, cute smile, always happy."

The receptionist nods. "Ah, right. You're looking for Nurse Siobhan Garrity. She has a little boy, not sure of his name to be honest as I don't know Nurse Garrity that well." Her face lights up. "She now works in the pulmonary vascular disease unit, but she's not in at the moment. Due in later." She checks her screen and nods.

"Oh, that's disappointing. I'm only here for the day. Do you have a contact number for her?" Despite trying my luck, the receptionist informs me that they do not give out personal contact details, but she can relay a message from me. I thank her for the offer but say I'll be back later as I'd like to give her these chocolates.

Back in my car, I glance around the car park watching cars cruise past searching for a space as I figure out my next move. It's a while before another idea springs to mind. Fishing my phone from my bag, I pull up Google and punch in nurseries in Cambridge. I groan as I see the list grow. "Think," I mutter. Then another thought comes to mind. Narrowing my search to those within a mile or two of the hospital might help. Siobhan probably needs a nursery close to work in case of an emergency.

It doesn't take long for the results to pop up and there are only five within a short walk to the hospital. *I must be crazy*. I dial the first number. Though the conversation starts well, and by that I mean the first thirty seconds, as soon as I ask if they have a Freddie Garrity, I'm told they cannot discuss anything to do with the children in their care. The next four calls end the same, and as I hang up for the last time I question what has come over me. Why would any nursery be stupid enough to confirm the name of a child in their care? For all they know I could be a deranged woman or an abductor. I throw my phone on to the passenger seat and run my hands through my hair.

This isn't going how I imagined. I rest my hands on the steering wheel and tap it furiously. I need to know what David is up to.

Another idea springs to mind and I hurry to put the key in the ignition and leave.

A few minutes later I pull up in the car park outside a small community hall that sits alongside the church in Hills Road. It's used by the church as a place where the local community can pop in for a cuppa and a biscuit,

The Ex-Husband

especially when it's cold outside. I sit in my car for a few minutes as I watch people come and go. A few elderly residents leaning on walking sticks potter in. To my right is a small gathering of dishevelled men standing in a circle a few feet away. My heart tugs at their situation. They have nowhere to go and no place to call home. For these rough sleepers, this is their only chance to grab a hot drink and free food during the day. I remember David saying the soup kitchen helped those living rough on the street both day and night.

Taking a deep breath, I step from my car and head into the building. A hive of activity and the low murmur of conversations filters around the room. They set up several tables with chairs around them. Towards the back is a row of tables with plates of biscuits and tea urns. Three volunteers stand behind the tables serving a small line of people. I look around but can't see David. I wonder if it's easier if I leave and return in a few hours. But then the growing need for answers pushes me forward. I approach the table of volunteers and catch the eye of a lady with a warm and pleasant smile. She must be in her sixties, maybe older.

"Hello dear. Can I get you a cup of tea?"

Her voice is soft, gentle, and calming like a still ocean. My nerves melt away as if I've had a cup of Camomile tea. "Not for me, thank you. Is David helping today? I can't see him." Glancing over my shoulder, I study the faces around the tables.

"David?" Her forehead creases.

"Oh, David Marchant. I know he helps with the soup kitchen in the centre of town. Is he helping here today?"

Recognition spreads across her face as her eyes widen. She nods. "He helps, but, his little boy has been unwell for a few days. Can I help?"

That sinking feeling washes over me again, the same one I felt as I walked away from the reception desk at the hospital.

Her eyes widen with concern. "I can get a message to him?"

"No, it's okay. I appreciate the offer anyway. Thank you." As I leave and head to my car, unease creeps into my bones. No one has seen David for a few days, and his sudden absence aligns with my police report. I don't know if that's a good or bad thing.

I started the search with hope, but as I sit in my car gazing at the same huddle of men I saw earlier, I feel deflated. David and his family are proving harder to track down than I imagined. I can go to the hospital again a bit later and try to speak to Siobhan. In the meantime, I don't know what to do. I grab my phone from my bag and call Anita. I'm desperate to hear her familiar voice and her reassuring thoughts. My call goes unanswered, and I reach her voicemail.

"Hi, Neets, it's only me. I'm missing you and could do with hearing your voice. Despite what you said about avoiding David, I need answers because I'm going through a tough time right now. Call me when you get a chance and I'll fill you in. Love you."

It's not like Anita to not pick up the phone. I can't remember the last time I left her a voicemail, and even if she didn't get to her phone quick enough, I'd always get a reply within seconds of hanging up. I redial her number and hold on for what feels like ages before I reach a voice-mail again. "Sorry, it's only me again. Hope you're okay. I guess you're busy."

I let out a deep sigh as I throw my phone back into my bag and start my car.

27

I RETURN to the hospital three hours later with my nerves on edge. It feels like an eternity since I was last here, and it takes every ounce of patience to not lurk in the corridors waiting for Siobhan. Parking is even more of a nightmare as the afternoon visiting hours lead to chaos in the hospital car park. If I wasn't already stressed, I am now, as I take over twenty minutes and a great deal of patience to find a parking space.

Every second counts as I hurry to the main doors and follow the signs to the pulmonary vascular disease unit. My heart is thundering in my chest like an old locomotive, but I'm not sure if that's from my anxiety or the fact that I jogged from the car to the hospital. The unit is ahead of me according to the signs hanging from the ceiling in the corridor. Visitors are milling about outside many of the wards, hushed conversations taking place. Nurses, doctors, and porters go about their jobs, weaving past me as they come out of one set of doors and dive into another. The familiar chime of an elevator heralds a patient being wheeled in a bed, her relatives trailing behind her.

There is so much happening around me, and it's hard to take it all in. When you add that to the smell of disinfectant that hangs in the air all around me, my senses feel overwhelmed.

I stop at the double doors to the unit and take a deep breath before stepping through. It's a hive of activity as I make my way to the nurses' desk and wait for a Filipino nurse to finish a call.

"Hi." The nurse places the handset in its cradle.

"Um... I wonder if you can help. I'm looking for Nurse Siobhan Garrity."

The nurse stands up and glances over the edge of the desk and looks in both directions. "She'll be in room C along the corridor."

I thank her and smile before following the directions. Room C houses four beds, all occupied. It's the female room with large windows which allows me to take a peek from the safety of the corridor. I spot a nurse taking off her plastic apron and stuffing it into a bin beside the sink at the end of the room. With no other nurse in the room, I take my chance and push through the doors, passing the four beds.

"Nurse Siobhan Garrity?"

The nurse turns around. She has a kind look about her, with a round, pretty face, freckles, and mousey brown hair tied back in a ponytail. Shorter than me, with a slim body.

"Yes, is everything okay?"

"Yes. I wonder if you can help." With one hand gripping the strap of my handbag, I shift on the spot, feeling the leather cutting into my palm. "I'm Jane Trebble. My ex-husband was David Marchant. I understand you're in a relationship with him. Can you spare me five minutes?"

Siobhan narrows her eyes and looks over my shoulder

The Ex-Husband 173

as she glances around the beds, before crossing her arms. "I'm sorry, but I'm working, and my personal life is just that, personal. I don't know who you are, so please can you leave?" Her stare is firm and final.

"I know this sounds odd, but I need to talk to you about David. There are things about him you might not know. Things about my marriage, and it might affect you. I need a few minutes, please? He's not the man you think he is, and it took every ounce of courage for me to get away from him. Please?" My voice is low so the patients can't hear.

Siobhan takes a step back, her jaw stiffens. She glares at me. "I won't ask you again. Please leave or I will call hospital security. I don't know what your problem is, but I can't help you."

Siobhan brushes past me and hurries out of the room. As I turn and follow her out, I realise that by the time I reach the corridor, she has vanished. I feel deflated but there is something in Siobhan's eyes that alarms me. I pace up and down the corridor glancing in the other rooms, but she's nowhere to be seen. Perhaps she has gone to call hospital security.

Not wishing to cause any more trouble, I make my way out of the unit and hurry back to my car. Shit. I feel my quest for the truth slipping through my fingers as more doors close around me. I'm running out of options.

Deep in thought, I clatter shoulders with visitors coming through the main doors.

"Watch where you're going!" a woman shouts. Her husband throws a protective arm around her as he tosses obscenities in my direction.

"I'm sorry." I scurry on, the woman still berating me.

"Jane!" a woman shouts behind me as I reach my car. When I spin round, Siobhan is hurrying towards me.

With both confusion and concern, I take a few steps back, my hands raised in surrender, avoiding any further confrontation.

"I'm sorry. I won't bother you again. Please don't call security."

Siobhan shakes her head and stops inches from me, before wrapping her arms around her waist. An awkward silence settles between us. Siobhan looks around the car park and then down at her feet before looking at me. "What did you want to tell me?"

I don't know where to begin without sounding like a lunatic. "I was married to David. It was an abusive relationship and the reason I left. I escaped and started a new life in Cambridge and then he reappeared when I spotted him in the city centre helping at a mobile soup kitchen. Since then, I've not been able to go anywhere or do anything without seeing him." The words tumble from my mouth and I'm not sure they even make sense, but I know I only have a few seconds before Siobhan loses interest and walks away. "I don't want him back in my life, so I'm not trying to take him from you, but he's told me he's a changed man and wants us to be friends again, even though you're all moving to Surrey for his new job. The church has given him a new purpose and he's settled into a new family life with you and your son, and that you are hoping to try for another baby. Is that all true?"

When I see Siobhan's eyes widen and I can't tell if it's surprise or fear. It's not the reaction I expected.

Siobhan shakes her head and blows out her cheeks. "God Almighty. I'm not in a relationship with David, nor am I moving to Surrey."

The revelation alone is enough to send me reeling.

She juts out a hip. "David asked me out after we met at

The Ex-Husband 175

church, but I refused. There was something about him I didn't like."

"What do you mean?" The words from Siobhan, each one heavier than the last, echo in the caverns of my mind, a chilling symphony of warnings I wished I heard sooner.

Siobhan grimaces and lets out a sigh. "I found David creepy. I found the way he looked at me very unsettling. Chilling actually. His eyes would bore into me, and the man didn't have to say one word for me to feel my insides turn. Of course he was very charming to everyone around him, especially in church, but I felt very uncomfortable being around him, even in the sanctuary of Sunday morning service. My son and I would stay for a cuppa after the service and it was nice to catch up with other parishioners. David was very good at working his way around the crowd. He pestered me for dates, but I kept turning him down. That's when things became difficult."

Heart thundering in my chest, I anticipate her next words. My mouth opens and then snaps closed again.

Siobhan hugs herself tighter as she stares at the floor. Her shoulders sag. "He began stalking me and it's the reason I switched churches. I told him to stay away from me or I'd call the police. As a single mum, I felt afraid for the safety of both me and my son."

I take a couple of minutes to process everything. David lied. Shit. "So all this stuff about being a changed man and having a family are lies. He even showed me a picture of you and Freddie."

Siobhan shakes her head. "What?"

I tell her again.

"I don't have a son called Freddie. My son is called Charlie. Whatever he told you about me and my son is a pack of lies. I never want to see that man again, and I've left a picture of David with hospital security in case he shows up here. This is my place of work, and I don't want to be looking over my shoulder expecting him to be there."

I'm left speechless as Siobhan stares at me for a few seconds and shrugs.

"Here is my number." I hand her a piece of paper. "If you want to talk further about it, then call me."

I watch her as she hurries away. My hands shake as I pull the phone out of my handbag, my mind swirling with confusion as the full extent of David's fixation and manipulation dawns on me. Bile rises and scorches my throat as I swallow it back down. "This can't be happening again," I mutter. I press Mark's number and wait for him to answer. I need to do something about David before he hurts me again.

28

I PACE round my lounge waiting for Mark to arrive. As I tried to tell him about my conversation with Siobhan, my message became garbled. Nonetheless, I think he understood most of it. He said he was making his way back and together we would decide what to do next. That was forty minutes ago. I check my phone in case I've missed a message from him before returning to the window once again and peering through the curtains. There is no sign of Mark or David, but it's my ex-husband I'm more worried about. He could be round the corner or pop up in his car further down the road.

My breathing is fast as my skin tingles. Desperate for Mark's return, I clench and unclench my free hand while stomping on the spot. I need to keep myself occupied, maybe cook something, or do the ironing, but nothing seems enticing enough to distract me. Aimlessly, I swipe the screen on my phone and scroll. It never ceases to amaze me how quickly time flies when you disappear down the rabbit hole of social media. Posts, videos, and adverts draw my attention away from the lounge window.

I've been doing this for ten or twenty minutes, perhaps longer, when I scream.

The news cuts through me and pierces my heart. I gasp for breath as I stagger backwards and fall on to the sofa. I'm still part of many Facebook groups from my hometown in Norfolk and a news report on one of them sends tears cascading from my eyes as if the dam wall has broken within me. It's a news report about a woman's body being found in her home and though the report is short, my breath catches in my throat when I recognise the photograph of the house.

It's Anita's.

Sobs wrack my body. Though I want to believe I'm mistaken and most houses around there look the same, I recognise distinguishable features which confirm my worst fears. I notice the boho inspired glass rainbow beads wind chime hanging inside her porch. The same wind chime I gave her for Christmas a few years ago. I recognise the tall bright orange flowerpots sitting either side of her front door. We chose them together at a craft fair. As I wipe the tears with the back of my hand, the news report confirms it's her street.

I curl up on the sofa and bury my head in a pillow as my body heaves with grief. I've lost my best friend. It would explain why she didn't return my calls. The thought occurs to me that she might have been injured at the time and unable to answer the phone. Could I have helped? Guilt washes over me.

The sound of a key in the door rattles me as I sit bolt upright to see Mark come in.

"Oh my God, what's the matter?" Mark's voice is laced with concern as I fall into his arms with sobs tearing from my throat.

The Ex-Husband 179

I gasped as I tried to talk. "It's... it's... Anita... She's dead. Oh my God. I can't... Why...?"

Mark grabs me by the shoulders and holds me away from his body to look at me. "Hold on a minute. Take a few deep breaths. What's happened?" He pushes my hair off my damp face.

I hold up my phone and show him the news article. He looks from the phone to me and then back again. His jaw drops in disbelief. "They don't know if it's suspicious or a tragic accident yet?" Mark scans through the article.

I nod. The word's not coming.

Mark leads me to the sofa and sits me down, dropping beside me and wrapping his arm around me.

"She was here recently, and now I'll never see her again." I break down as sobs shake my body. There's nothing Mark can say to make it better as he holds me tight.

"We'll get in touch with the local force to find out more. They may want to talk to you anyway because you are..." Mark pauses for a moment, "were her best friend. They'll be able to build a better picture of Anita if they speak to you."

I nod as I sniff. "Mark, what happens if David did this? He hated Anita. I saw the look in his eye when she confronted him in town during her visit. He's hated Anita ever since she helped me to get away. And no one has seen him for the last few days. What if it was him?"

Mark shakes his head. "That's a big assumption, Jane."

It is a big assumption, and maybe I'm being paranoid, but my gut instinct tells me that David played a part in it. He has never reacted well to anyone challenging him. I should know.

I pull myself away from Mark and get up to fetch a tissue before taking my spot by the lounge window again.

My house and street used to represent freedom and now they feel claustrophobic. Everything I've done to build up my new life here seems to have crumbled around my feet and it's all David's fault. Bit by bit he is eroding my identity and my life again. And now I don't even have Anita for steadfast support. A constant and my rock through the darkest days, and now she's gone.

Turning to Mark, I lean back and rest my head. "I need to speak to the police. I need to tell them what Siobhan told me, and how he's been lying to everyone. That has to lend weight to my concerns?"

Mark nods in agreement.

"If he's lied about having a family, what else has he lied about? Has he got a new job in Surrey? Where has he been for the last few days? Once I tell them about his confrontation with Anita a few days ago, and their history, they must take my concern seriously?"

Mark shrugs. "You would think so. Give the DC a call and ask for a meeting."

I gather myself together and nod before picking up my phone and dialling.

"Detective Constable Jess Carter," she answers.

"Detective, this is Jane Trebble, about my ex-husband David Marchant."

"Yes, Jane. I remember. How can I help?"

"I need to make an appointment with you urgently. I've found out that everything David told me is a lie about his new life here, and the woman he claimed is his partner isn't. He stalked her as well."

"Okay, I understand. And you'd like to come in and see me?"

"Yes, tomorrow morning, if possible?"

There's a pause on the other end of the line and I hear

The Ex-Husband 181

the rustling of paper and what sounds like the clicking of a mouse. "I can do nine-thirty. Is that good for you?"

"Yes, thank you, detective. I'll see you tomorrow."

I call Kathy, my HR manager, to tell her about Anita and my appointment with the police tomorrow morning. She completely understands and asks me to keep her in the loop and suggests that I take some time off as compassionate leave. I appreciate her concern and once I'm finished with her, I have the same conversations with Brad, my director, and Georgia. Brad sounds concerned and tells me not to worry and they'll manage.

It's my call with Georgia that's the most difficult. I don't know who's the more upset, me or her. My heartstrings tug as she chokes on her tears when I tell her I won't be in for a while.

29

MY EYES ARE tired and sore this morning. Pictures of Anita flash in front of my eyes. I'm not even sure I had much sleep last night. I went from periods of sitting up in bed and crying, to going downstairs and drinking cups of tea, before curling up on the sofa and flicking through my photo gallery on my phone.

Has she really gone? Despite seeing it on the news last night, it still seems hard to believe. With Anita by my side, I felt stronger; however, now that she's no longer on this earth, I feel weaker. As my eyes water once more, I sniff and use the back of my hand to wipe away the dampness.

Mark groans and rolls over in bed to face me. "Are you okay?"

"I guess. I can't believe she's gone. What am I going to do, Mark?"

"I know it hurts. And with so much happening, it's overwhelming. But I am here for you. I'll do whatever I can to help."

I purse my lips and look at Mark. The thought of losing him makes me feel sick. It's not like we've been together for years, but he holds such a significant place in my life, and the thought of him not being around is too much for me to bear.

Mark sits up in bed and rubs sleep from his eyes. "First thing you need to do after breakfast is to get yourself ready for your appointment with the detective. Are you sure you don't want me to come with you? I don't mind."

"Thanks. But this is something I need to do for myself. I've reached the stage where my shadow scares me and every sound in the house puts me on high alert. I can't carry on living life like this. Taking back control is something I owe to myself and Anita." Even as those words leave my lips, I'm wondering if I'm strong enough to take back control.

Mark throws the duvet back. "I'm going to grab a quick shower. Is that okay?"

"Sure. I'll put the kettle on. Do you want toast?" I ask, sliding my feet out of the bed and putting on my dressing gown.

"That would be lovely... as long as you chuck on a load of jam." Mark throws me a wink.

I leave Mark in the shower as I head downstairs, and when I get to the last step I see the postman has been already. *Early for him*, I think. I pick up the white A4 envelope and flip it over to see my name on the front, a square of paper with my name typed on it and then stuck to the front. There's nothing else on it, not even a postmark. This was hand delivered. I slide my finger under the flap and open it to find a sheet of paper and white fabric in the bottom of the envelope.

With my curiosity piqued, I pull out the paper and the fabric. My eyes widen with shock, and I freeze on the spot, my body rigid with fear. It's a pair of white knickers from

Victoria's Secret, and identical to the ones I have upstairs in my underwear drawer. I'm filled with a mixture of surprise and confusion, but as I read the message, my blood runs cold.

Roses are red.
Violets are blue.
Ur window is open.
I'm climbing through.
Everyone is asleep.
And u are too.
I'm in ur bedroom.
Watching you!
x

"Mark!" I scream as I race back up the stairs and into the bathroom.

"Mark!" I scream again.

"What?" Mark jumps in the shower and spins round. Shampoo suds streak across his face.

"Someone is watching me. I think they've been in my house."

"What are you talking about?"

I show Mark the envelope and its contents, reading out the message to him as he rinses the suds off him. I can tell he's as shocked as me as his mouth falls open, the steam from the shower encasing us in a warm mist.

"Shit, you need to get this to the police. Put everything back in the envelope." Mark steps out and grabs his towel to dry off.

I'm already doing it as I hurry from the bathroom to my bedroom and head straight to my chest of drawers. I pull everything out of the top drawer and search for my white Victoria's Secret knickers. I remember they came as a pack of three. I find the first one and throw it on the bed. Seconds later, I find the second pair. I'm frantic as I'm like a beaver burrowing through the soil. I can't find the third pair. They're not in the wash basket as I did a white wash two days ago. Where are they? *Please, God, no!* I stop and stare at my empty drawer. Mark comes in and stops in the doorway, casting his eye over the mess I've created around me on the floor.

With a chilling realisation, I look at Mark as my mouth runs dry and my body trembles. "It's my knickers," is all I can whisper before I clutch the sides of my head. My eyes search wildly around the room. "Someone broke into my house. Mark! Someone got in!" I scream.

Mark throws his arms around me as he tries to calm me down. I'm a bag of nerves now knowing that someone has invaded my personal space.

"Shit, Mark. They got into my house."

"How? There are no signs of forced entry. The windows and doors are intact."

I shrug. I don't have the answers. But I'm confused and also bloody terrified.

Mark steps back and surveys the heaps of underwear around us. "Did you leave your keys lying around at work? Or on the table while you've been out with your friends from work?"

I shake my head. "I always leave my keys in my bag. Besides, I can't imagine anyone from work doing this?"

Mark studies my features. "Do you leave your bag unattended?"

"I do. But it's only when I'm going to make a cup of tea or go to the toilet. It's an open-plan office. I know all of them. If anyone was going through my bag, the others would spot it straight away."

"It only takes a second," he reminds me, and I know he's right. These are the same questions the detective will ask me, and I know how it's going to look. I leave my bag

The Ex-Husband **187**

unattended every day while I go to the toilet or kitchen. Most people do, right? Or is it me?

At first, I was scared, but now I'm petrified as I dress for my appointment, all the while peeking from my bedroom window every few minutes for anything unusual outside.

Upon waiting in reception for only a few minutes, the door to my left opens and Detective Constable Jess Carter appears, greeting me with a small smile.

"Jane, sorry to keep you waiting. Would you like to follow me?"

"That's okay. I've not been waiting long." I rise and follow her through the same doors that we went through during my last visit, but on this occasion we venture further into the police station and end up in another interview suite. It's larger than the last one and comfier too. It has two beige sofas, a few prints on the wall, and a dark brown carpet. I notice a small camera hanging from the ceiling in one corner.

"Thank you for seeing me, detective."

Jess smiles and opens her notepad. "Not a problem. Can I get you a tea or coffee, or a glass of water?"

"No, thank you."

"I understand you want to talk to me about your ex-husband, David?"

"Yes, as I mentioned on the phone yesterday, I discovered that everything David has been telling me is a lie." I spend the next few minutes telling her about my conversation with Siobhan Garrity and how she has never been in a relationship with David and switched churches to get away from his unwanted attention. All the while I'm talking, the detective makes notes while looking up at me and offering words of encouragement.

I pause as tears fill my eyes. "Something else happened. Yesterday, I found out that my best friend was found dead at her home in Norfolk. I saw the news report online. I tried to contact her prior to that. It was odd that she didn't answer, considering she's quick to pick up her phone."

Detective Jess Carter's face becomes serious for a moment. "I'm sorry to hear that."

"David had something to do with it. We had a run-in with him when she came to visit me and I could tell he wasn't happy at being challenged by her. Anita was the main reason I could escape my marriage and start a new life here. David hated her interfering in our lives, and I remember him one day saying that the bitch will regret ever crossing him."

"I'll have to make a few enquiries with my colleagues in Norfolk, as I'm not familiar with that case. But you think David may have had a part to play in her death?"

"I don't know. The news report said the police were treating the death as suspicious. So maybe, yes."

"Can you provide any other supporting evidence, such as recorded messages, witnesses, or past records, that imply David's involvement in your friend's death?"

Shit. I have nothing other than my gut feeling. The detective waits for an answer, but I have nothing to give her as I let out a sigh.

"Was Siobhan able to give you any contact details for David?"

"Sorry, I didn't ask. But she's a nurse at the Royal Papworth Hospital."

"Not to worry. I'll get in touch with the hospital. Following your last visit, I ran a preliminary search on his

The Ex-Husband 189

name and only discovered an address for him in Norfolk. I'll run further checks with mobile phone providers and the council. In addition, I'll visit the church, as you mentioned he works at the gift shop. I would imagine they have contact details for him."

"Thank you. There's something else I need to show you." I reach into my bag and pull out the white A4 envelope. "I received this earlier today." Resting it on the table, I remove the letter and unfold it. There's a tremor in my fingers as I pull out my knickers from the envelope. Every part of me wants to cry and scream. The sight of my underwear leaves me with a sense of violation and embarrassment.

The detective looks at both, taking a moment to read the rhyme, before looking back at me.

"Somehow, someone has got into my house and stolen my knickers. I had three pairs of these. There were only two in my underwear drawer."

Detective Carter furrows her brow. "Did someone break in?"

"No. All my windows and doors are intact and not damaged. My boyfriend checked this morning."

Detective Carter looks perplexed as she purses her lips. "Can you think of any situation where someone might have taken your keys and potentially copied them?"

In the same way that I explained to Mark this morning, I tell the detective how I leave my bag beside me on the floor while working. She asks if I've had any uncomfortable or unusual encounters at work or outside work, to which I reply no other than David, and hence the reason I'm so worried.

I sit in silence, wringing my hands as the detective finishes her notes. All the while I gaze around the room and wrack my brains over who could have copied my keys without me knowing. The only other person who has access to my spare keys is Mark, but I think I know him well enough to know that he's not the type of person to do something like this.

"Okay, Jane. I think I have everything. I'll keep these as evidence if that's okay and I'll call the senior investigating officer dealing with your friend's case and I'll also see if I can track down the whereabouts of your ex-husband." The detective pauses as she stares at her notes. "And you're sure there are no signs of a break-in?"

"Not that we can see."

"Right, I'll arrange for a local neighbourhood officer to pop in today to check all your doors and windows for you. We need to check if anyone has tampered with any locks."

I thank her and welcome the reassurance,

"Can you also email me the name of your HR manager? I'd like to keep them in the loop as I'll need the names of all your colleagues, so I can run checks on them."

Her suggestion alarms me. "Could someone be stalking me at work?"

"I don't know. It's possible. We have to consider all angles. That your bag is left unattended provides ample opportunity for someone to borrow your keys and get a set cut."

My chest tightens. Everyone is under suspicion now.

"I'd also suggest that you get your front and rear door locks changed as a priority," the detective stresses as she rests her elbows on her knees. "I know I've said this before, but please stay vigilant. If there's anything that you notice that's odd, or if you see David around town again, please call me at once. You have my mobile number. I'll give you an update as soon as I have more for you."

I wait while the detective pops outs of the room to

grab an evidence bag and nitrile gloves to secure the envelope and its contents. She returns moments later, and I watch her snap on the gloves and place the items in a brown paper bag. She writes my name on the front and dates it.

With that, she rises from her sofa and shows me out of the station. It's a short walk to the visitors' car park, where she waits for me to leave before waving me off. As the image of Detective Jess Carter disappears from my rearview mirror, I feel a sense of relief knowing that the police are taking my concern seriously. My only fear is David is still out there somewhere and until I know where, I'll be on edge day and night.

30

THERE WAS something quite special about seeing Jane's reaction when she opened my envelope. I couldn't help but afford myself a little smile, but once again, I wished my video feed had sound but that would have meant larger cameras with built-in mics, and they would have been harder to hide.

As I replay that moment again, I rock back and forth in my chair. I freeze-frame at the precise moment when a look of horror spreads across her face. It is in marked contrast to how she looks, and that is something that excites me.

Though my room is dark with only the illumination from the screen throwing a faint glow around it, I glance up at the corkboard hanging from the wall to my right and cast my gaze across the many images of Jane. Photographs taken in happier times. Socialising with friends. Work Christmas parties. Wandering around the shops laden with bags. Tending the garden in the summer wearing a white T-shirt, cut-down denim shorts, and flip-flops.

I sigh.

As much as I want to continue watching her from afar and on my live feeds, I need to tell her how I feel.

31

I'M NOT aware of my surroundings as I drive home. My meeting with Detective Constable Jess Carter races through my mind. Her words were clear: "Unless he has broken the law and physically assaulted you, made physical threats, or intimidated you, then there is very little we can do other than pay him a visit to explain the distress he is causing you."

That's what worries me. David is being very careful. I know he hasn't harmed me or outright threatened me with violence, but his presence alone is enough to terrify me. There's a certain look in his eye that I've grown used to. And whenever I see it I'm taken back to when he controlled me. I don't think anyone can understand the pain and trauma it causes unless they've been on the receiving end of it.

Everyone experiences it differently. For me, it was very surreal. I became very disconnected over time, and empty inside, like my body was a shell. I can still recall the sensations I had when the violence was taking place. It was terrifying. In fact, it was almost like it was so terrifying that I could not sense anything within myself. I remember waking up each morning wondering if the events of the day before had happened.

And it was so subtle to begin with that it wasn't noticeable. I realise that now. It was small things that sounded good at the time. "Please don't go out with your friends tonight. I love you and miss you so much when you are out." At the time, it didn't sound manipulative to me, but I realise it was.

I now regret making excuses for his behaviour, and the number of times I told myself that, "it wasn't that bad really." Or, "it was my fault, I provoked him." Or, "he's having a hard time at work, and he said he won't do it again, he promised."

"Idiot," I mutter as I slow down at the lights. I'll never get those years back and the memories will haunt me forever, but I can't and won't let this happen again. Just David's presence in Cambridge has wiped out all the good I've done to rebuild my life and to regain my confidence. Bastard. And though I can't prove it, I have a gut feeling that David had some part to play in Anita's death. But how did he break into my house if he was the one who stole my underwear? Mark checked, there was no damage to any window or door. That's something that still confuses me.

The rest of the journey feels like a blur as I turn into my street and head towards my house. This has been my sanctuary. A place where I healed, but now I'm filled with the unease that flutters in my stomach as I pull on to my drive. There's not much to see as I step out of my car and check my surroundings. There's no one around, and I can't see David's car. That's a blessing, though I can't help but notice the slight tremor in my left hand as I fumble for my door keys. And the harder I try to unlock my door, the clumsier I become as I stumble through the open door. I

The Ex-Husband 197

slam it shut behind me and double-lock it before heading into the lounge and throwing my bag on the sofa.

I take up my usual spot by the lounge window and check again. Mark has pulled me up on this a few times, but my nerves get the better of me. I can sense my pulse thumping in my ears as I turn and head towards the kitchen to put on the kettle.

My hand stops mid-air as the mundane act of reaching for a mug twists into a swirl of dread. A gasp, more felt than heard, ripples through the silence of the kitchen, my body becoming frozen in horror.

David materialises from the stillness, not simply a man but a manifestation of every unspoken fear, a chilling spectre in the flesh. The space between us crackles with the raw intensity of a storm about to break. The kitchen— a place once synonymous with comfort—now the backdrop for a terrifying reckoning. Every horrific thing he could do to me plays before my eyes like a movie reel.

His piercing gaze unravels the very fabric of my being. The atmosphere becomes electrified, a tangible dread that envelops me, refusing passage. In this moment, David transcends the bounds of my most harrowing nightmares, his figure a dark imposition against the feeble kitchen light.

This man's mere presence is a stark reminder that nowhere, not even within these walls, am I safe from the shadows of my past.

I back away as far as I can go before the kitchen cupboards jam up against my legs. "Stay away!" I scream.

David's expression is stony, his icy eyes boring into me. It's the same look I've seen a thousand times. The one he keeps for special occasions behind closed doors. My blood runs cold as my fingers grip the worktop behind me.

"That's no way to treat your husband. You know what

happens when you speak to me like that," he whispers, his voice steady and flat as he moves to block the doorway to the lounge.

I jab a finger in his direction. "You're not my husband any more. Get out or I'll call the police."

"That's a bit of paper. I'll always be your husband. No one can replace me. And you will always be my wife until death do us part. Why do you think I came to find you? I'm here to take you back to Norfolk with me." He takes one step towards me.

"Stay away," I growl.

"Jane. Enough. This time had to come. I found you weeks ago and have been following you since. I know where you go, what you do with *him*, where you work, what shops you go to. I've sat in that café across the road from your work and waited hours. Every time you left the building, I was close to you. How else do you think I *bumped* into you?" He smiles and looks at me like a lovesick teenager. "I've even watched you through your kitchen window in the evening."

My breath is choppy and raw, my eyes wide with fear. "Get away from me! I swear if you lay a finger on me, I'll kill you. You can't hurt me any more. I'm not playing your games. I know everything you've said to me is a lie. Your make-believe family doesn't exist. I've spoken to Siobhan. And the police know all about it. That's where I've just been. They are out looking for you now."

David's smile tugs at his lips. "I'll take you back to Norfolk with me before they find us. I have a little remote cottage in the middle of nowhere. Just you and me. No Internet and no distractions. We can start all over. It can be like old times again. I can help you choose what to wear. You can cook for me like you used to. We can make

The Ex-Husband 199

love whenever the mood takes us. You forget my exacting attention to every detail, Jane."

David storms towards me, and I sidestep him as I race around the kitchen table to escape. He yells as he kicks away the chairs in his way and pursues me through the lounge towards the front door. I scramble for the keys cursing myself for double-locking the door. But it's too late as David catches up. He grabs me by the hair and yanks me back. A searing hot and burning pain spreads across my scalp. I bare my teeth and cry in pain as he drags me back into the lounge and throws me on to the sofa.

I gasp for breath as panic tightens my throat and squeezes my chest till it feels like there's a stack of bricks pressing down on me. "Please! Stop!" I plead as I try to push him away.

He stands over me, his eyes burning into me, his face red and twisted with rage. "Don't. Ever. Do. That. Again."

And as quickly as that, the creases in his face smooth out and the softness returns, replacing his rage. He leans forward and strokes my hair. "I'm sorry. I love you so much. And it's my love for you that makes me do these crazy, crazy things. I don't think you realise how much you mean to me."

My fists tighten in defiance. "You're a fucking lunatic. Stay away from me. You can't control me any more. You have no power over me. This ends now. I can't prove it, but I know you had something to do with Anita's death. That's why you haven't been around for a few days. No one has seen you. You went to Norfolk didn't you?"

David's eyes widen in surprise. "What? I don't know what you're talking about. Anita is dead? Well, I'm not surprised."

I jump up from the sofa, a surge of anger swelling

inside me. I glare at him and stab a finger into his chest. "You hated her. She threatened you, and you didn't like that. Go on, be a man for a change, admit it."

David continues to protest his innocence, and as he looks around the lounge, I inch away from him and towards the lounge window. I think if I can get to the window, I can attract someone's attention. I pray Mark will be here any second, and if I can keep David talking, it will buy me enough time.

"There's nothing to admit," he rants. "Besides, it doesn't matter anyway. That old witch is nothing to me. She's nothing to *us!* She deserved it whatever happened to her. Interfering cow. We were fine until she butted her nose into our business."

I think of what to say, but the words don't come. All I can think of is to keep inching away from him.

But my plan is thrown into disarray as David flips again, the rage consuming him. "Don't you dare move," he snarls as he pulls out a knife from the inside of his jacket pocket.

I scream as I throw my hands to my chest and back away. "Please, David. Don't do this. You are only making things worse. Why are you doing this? Can't you see how much trouble you're causing for yourself? It doesn't have to end like this. You can meet someone else. You can start again. Please go. Move to the other end of the country if you want. I promise I won't tell anyone."

"Shut up, my darling Jane. There is no one else. No one understands me like you do. Can't you see that we are meant for each other, my darling Jane? No one else will love you the way I love you. I loved you from the moment I saw you. And I know you felt the same. But you've forgotten that you need to listen to me. I need to put you back in line. Your time away from me has given you a

The Ex-Husband

foolish dose of courage. I need to make you remember how much you love me."

"I don't love you any more, David. You stole my chance of happiness when you kicked the love out of me a long time ago. You destroyed our baby because of your actions. You didn't want a wife, but a punchbag and obedient servant. Someone to control because you thrive on it. You took away my identity and stripped me of my personality, and left me without friends, family, career, and a life. But you're a pathetic and weak excuse of a man who doesn't deserve to be called a husband ever again."

"Bitch!" he yells. David charges towards me.

I can't remember what I feel first. The force of my head hitting the wall as he shoves me back, or the knife cutting my flesh. I scream as a bolt of pain shoots down my arm. I lower my gaze and notice the blood seeping through my clothes, and I experience light-headedness as shock overwhelms me.

David grabs my head and slams it against the wall again. Though my vision blurs, an animal instinct to survive drives me on as I rake my nails down his face. He screams and drops the knife as he clutches his face. It's my chance. I lunge for the knife, getting to it before him, but as I wave it in front of him, he lunges at me again and with all his might shoves me in the chest. I tumble back and collide with the wall. My legs go weak as I slide down the wall to the floor.

"You will not get away from me again! You belong to me and will always belong to me!" David yells as he pulls out his phone from his back pocket and dials 999.

Everything around me spins as my vision blurs. A warm trickle of blood drips from my fingers.

"Hello, I need the police. My ex-wife has gone crazy and stabbed me. I need help. I'm bleeding."

My eyelids flicker as I struggle to make sense of what I've heard. Did I get the words jumbled up? Maybe he said I stabbed my ex-wife. I can't be certain as I turn and focus on David. He glares at me with a twisted smile on his face. I gasp and yell as he plunges the knife into his thigh not once, but twice, before staggering forward. He leans forward and grabs my hand, wrapping my bloodied fingers around the handle. But I'm too weak to resist as I feel waves of nausea washing through me.

David staggers towards the front door and unlocks it before smearing his bloodied fingers down it. He opens the door and drops into the doorway. "You stabbed me you crazy bitch!" he screams in agony as he clutches his leg. "Help! You're bloody dangerous and unstable."

The sound of his voice fades out as my vision goes dark.

32

I HEAR noises from somewhere deep within me. Mumbles more than anything else, but as I come round, my senses tune into words being spoken.

"Help! She stabbed me."

"Jesus, shit!"

The voice swirls around me and I take a few moments to realise that it's not one voice, but two. My eyes flicker open as I struggle to notice who is here and where I am. I'm in my lounge slumped against the wall and the voices are from the doorway to my right.

A voice still screams for help, but then I hear the familiar voice of Mark. He rushes to me and takes my hand.

"Oh, God. Please. No." Mark brushes away my damp matted hair that clings to my face. I can hear more voices now. The commotion. The panic.

When I look at Mark, it seems like I'm peering through foggy glass and nothing appears clear. I groan as I whisper his name.

"Sssh, try not to talk. I'm calling for help." Mark places his phone to his ear and calls for an ambulance.

"Mark." I'm barely able to get the word out as tears squeeze from my eyes. "He tried to kill me."

"I know. It's going to be okay. Help is on its way."

I lose track of time as I hear more voices gather by the door, and a few other people join Mark as they crowd around me. The more I try to push the words out, the more Mark tells me to rest. It's not long before I hear approaching sirens, and then the footsteps of help.

"Okay, can I have everyone leave the room please? Let's make a bit of room." The ambulance paramedic takes charge as she ushers people out of the way. Her voice blends into the cacophony of sounds flooding through my front door. David's screams, panicked voices, more sirens.

"I need to stay. I'm her boyfriend." Mark remains rooted to the spot as he clutches my hand.

All of a sudden my lounge feels like it's a tiny box room as further ambulance personnel and police officers arrive and fill the space.

"You're going to be okay," a paramedic reassures me as she applies gauze and bandages to the deep laceration on my arm. My head pounds as sweat beads from my forehead. Waves of nausea rush through me.

"Does it hurt anywhere else?" the female paramedic asks as she shines a light from her torch in my eyes.

I nod, but the muscles in my neck feel weak and sore. "My head. He banged my head against the wall a few times. I feel sick."

"Okay, love. You may have a bit of concussion. We'll get you into the ambulance so we can do a proper assessment before taking you to hospital. You'll be fine." The

The Ex-Husband 205

paramedic instructs a colleague to get a spinal board and neck brace.

I swallow past the lump in my throat. "He tried to kill me."

"Let's get you sorted first. Don't worry about anything. The police are here. Once you're in the ambulance and we have you stable, you can speak to them."

I haven't got the strength to reply as the paramedics manoeuvre me from my prone position against the wall to the spinal board before covering me in a blanket. As they lift and take me through the door, I can still hear David protesting his innocence and his claims that I attacked him. I want to dispute them. Although I want to undo the straps holding me in and jump off the spinal board to confront David face to face, I'm too weak and exhausted. He attacked me. They have to believe me.

Away from the noise and commotion outside my house I sense a crowd gathering on the pavement. I see faces in the crowd, confirming my suspicions as my eyes dart left to right.

"Oh my God, Jane. What on earth has happened?" Chrissy chokes on her words as she rushes to me and places her hand on my arm. She gives me a soft squeeze. I'm too tired to smile or acknowledge her. Shock has left me exhausted and numb. As I gaze up at the sky, grey and lifeless, mirroring my emotions, I don't understand how it has come to this.

"You're going to be okay. I'm by your side." Mark is close by and places his hand on my leg as he catches up. I feel a degree of warm comfort and reassurance knowing he's still here.

Inside the ambulance and with the door shut, the cold and sterile atmosphere replaces the drama of what's taking place outside. The paramedic checks my vital statistics while her colleague gathers background information from Mark to fill in their forms.

"You're lucky. The laceration on your arm isn't too deep. There doesn't appear to be any damage to the major arteries. Can you feel this?" the paramedic asks. She jabs the tip of each finger on my right hand with a small needle to check the numbness.

I nod.

"That's good. The doctors can take a proper look at this, although you'll only need stitches. They can check for any nerve damage."

Mark smiles at me and winks as he stands to one side, his arms folded across his chest. I can see the worry on his face. His eyes are wide and fixed, his lips pursed tight. It's a relief to hear those words because the throbbing in my arm appears to be getting worse. Perhaps the adrenaline wearing off is causing a spike in my pain and tiredness in my body.

The side door of the ambulance opens and a police officer steps in. He takes a seat opposite me and casts his eye over Mark and then me before he offers a friendly smile. "I'm PC Jarvis. How are you feeling?"

"Okay." There's no more I can say.

"We'll interview you at the hospital if you're up to it, but can you remember much of what happened?"

The constable takes his pen and pad from a pouch on his stab jacket in readiness to take down anything I might say. My eyes narrow, the glare from the lights above me too bright. "I... I... came home. Um..." My mind feels confused. I struggle to join the dots and explain my movements after coming home. "I went to the kitchen to make myself a cup of tea." My eyes jump around as if they're doing an Irish jig as I track back through my memories. "I turned and David was standing there behind the kitchen door."

PC Jarvis looks down at his notepad and runs his hand through his short, dark brown hair. He looks weathered and tired, as if years on the job and the violence and tragedy he's witnessed has taken its toll on him. He sighs louder than he expected, and glances at me before returning to his notes. "David Marchant? I understand he is your ex-husband?"

"Yes. I tried to get away from him and escape. But I had locked the door, and he caught up with me. He attacked me and smashed my head against the wall before stabbing me." I pause for a few moments. I'm sure there must be more I can say to him, but my mind is in a state of disarray, and I can't gather my thoughts. Recollections seem vague.

"Okay." The constable jots down a few notes. "I understand talking to one of my colleagues, DC Jess Carter, that you've complained about being stalked by your ex-husband?"

"Yes. I moved to Cambridge to get away from him and my abusive marriage."

"So you didn't invite him in?"

"No." I reply adamantly, annoyed at the insinuation. "He was already there. He must have broken in."

"My colleagues are checking your property now for any signs of forced entry. They are also taking witness statements. We'll need one from you while it's fresh in your mind." The constable looks towards Mark. Mark nods but says nothing.

There's a knock on the door before it opens, and another officer appears. He gestures to PC Jarvis to join him outside. While they're gone, Mark comes towards me and kisses me on the forehead. "You're doing really well. Do you need anything?"

"No. My arm is throbbing."

"I can give you painkillers for that," the paramedic chips in. She rises from her chair and searches the small cupboard above me.

It's only another minute or two before PC Jarvis steps back into the ambulance and takes a seat opposite me. His face takes on a serious expression. "David Marchant has made an accusation that you invited him over to talk about a reconciliation. He claims when he turned you down, you attacked him with a knife. We have recovered a knife from the scene and forensic services will be here soon."

His words sting and I can't believe I'm hearing this. I glance at Mark who looks as confused.

"No, he attacked Jane," Mark interrupts as he points a finger in my direction. "Jane is the victim here. That man is dangerous. Why do you think Jane went to the police with proof multiple times? If you'd done your job and found him, this would not have happened." Mark glares at the police officer who remains stony-faced.

PC Jarvis looks at me and raises a hand. "This is standard procedure. I'm not taking sides here. You're accusing him, and he's accusing you. So officers will interview you formally from CID. So before you say anything and for your protection, Jane Trebble, you do not have to say anything. But, it may harm your defence if you do not mention when questioned something which you later rely on in court. Anything you do say may be given in evidence."

"No. This can't be right!" I shout. "He attacked *me* in my home. He stabbed himself to make it look like I attacked him." The suggestion sounds ridiculous as it leaves my lips, and I wonder what PC Jarvis must be thinking.

"I don't doubt that. The fact is that both of you have been injured." PC Jarvis pauses for a moment to look at me. His eyes are soft even though his voice is direct and lacks warmth. "With the discovery of a weapon, we have to work out what's happened and take formal statements from both of you under caution. As soon as you're discharged from the hospital, and if you're fit to be interviewed, one of my colleagues in CID will arrange for you to attend the police station for an interview." PC Jarvis rises from his seat. "Sorry. I'm not being hard on you. I'm following procedure. We have not yet apportioned blame to either party. We need the facts first."

I lie there dumbfounded. My mouth hangs open as I watch PC Jarvis exit the ambulance. I turn to Mark. He reaches for my hand and gives it a squeeze. "Don't worry. You have done nothing wrong. Once he's spoken to DC Jess Carter in more detail, they'll know he's lying."

"Or they might think that I had planned all of this, including talking to the police before I attacked him."

"Don't be silly, Jane. No one thinks that."

In the back of my mind I'm not so sure. In public David hasn't put a foot wrong. His work with the church, helping at the mobile soup kitchen, and even charming Chrissy, my neighbour. Will they believe anything I say?

33

I DIDN'T SLEEP VERY WELL last night, and neither did Mark. There was no way I could return to my house, so I went back to Mark's in the early hours of the morning. I wake earlier than him and sit on the sofa cradling a cup of tea, feeling more like a criminal than a victim. While I was being treated, Detective Constable Carter came to the hospital to check on my condition. Once the doctors stitched me up and gave me painkillers, I went with her to the police station where she formally interviewed me.

The memory of last night weighs on my mind. I was attacked in my own home but the police interviewed me as a suspect in the violent assault on David. His version of events yesterday conflicted with mine and the detective wanted to go through the sequence of events which led up to Mark discovering the aftermath.

They interviewed Mark as well to gain his perspective but kept us separate. I wanted to see him, but they wouldn't allow it until both interviews were complete. The police remained at my house for hours after the attack. Crime scene investigators gathered evidence from the lounge and hallway and also examined all my windows and doors for signs of forced entry. Officers informed me that someone had gained access to my house through a rear window, which further supported my story of David attacking me, but they gave me the usual line that the investigation was still ongoing.

How did it come to this? They released me pending further enquiries. David remains in hospital having undergone minor surgery on the stab wounds to his leg. I only wish they were fatal. Then perhaps this horrible nightmare could be behind me.

My phone vibrates on the sofa beside me. I glance at the screen but don't recognise the number. "Hello?" There's silence on the line for a few seconds before a hesitant voice replies.

"Um. Jane. It's Siobhan Garrity. I saw the local news last night and your name being mentioned. Are you okay?"

I'm taken aback by her call. I never expected to hear from her. "Yes. I'm okay. It's been a tough few hours."

"I'm sure it has. Was it David?"

I close my eyes and shiver at the mention of his name. I nod and say yes.

"Shit. What's happening with the police?"

I take a few moments to tell her about my claims and his counterclaims, and my police interview. She offers words of encouragement and support. Even though she was frosty with me when we met at the hospital, and I don't blame her for that, there's a softness in her tone now, one that I think carries compassion and concern. I thank her for her call and for her offer of help before hanging up.

"Who was that?" Mark comes into the lounge and rubs the sleep from his eyes.

"Siobhan Garrity. She saw the local news and my name being mentioned. Funny how they never mention David's name. And now everyone knows my business. And if they arrest or charge me with GBH or attempted murder, then my life is over." I bury my head in my hands.

Mark sits beside me and wraps his arm around my shoulder and pulls me into his chest. I lay my head on him. I feel so lost and confused. After so many years of turmoil I was back in control, but now it seems like my life is falling apart. I don't know what to think. Losing Anita was bad enough, but Detective Constable Carter dropped a bombshell on me last night. She spoke to her colleagues in Norfolk. The investigating team is treating Anita's death as murder and not as a tragic accident. A forensic sweep of her property led to the discovery of marks on her rear kitchen window, which suggested a blunt instrument was used to gain access to her house.

I know in my heart that David is responsible, but pleading with the detective last night only made me sound like a mad woman. David hated Anita and swore she would pay the price for interfering in his marriage. I'm certain Anita paid with her life. Detective Carter mentioned that officers from Norfolk would interview David as part of their investigation. That was good to hear, but she questioned me at length about my own attack. She kept pressing me on how we fought in the kitchen and lounge. In their eyes, they could have viewed my attack on him as premeditated and me planning this all along to appear as a victim of harassment.

"How are you feeling?"

Without much thought, I shrug. The honest answer is that I don't know. My emotions are confused and I'm unsure of what to believe. I've received a string of messages and many calls from concerned friends. Georgia was in tears when she called earlier this morning. Brad Ritchie, my boss, was just as concerned when he called too. While I recover, they have given me indefinite leave. I should feel relieved, but if anything, I feel worse.

"Do you want anything?" Mark asks, kissing the top of my head as he runs a hand up and down my arm.

"Clothes, but I can't face going back to my house alone."

"I can come with? You can grab what you need and stay here for a while. It would be nice to look after you for a change."

He's lovely and so considerate that I agree, peeling myself away from him. "Can I grab a shower before we go? I smell of hospitals and disinfectant."

"Sure, no problem. How are you going to keep your arm dry?"

"Not sure," I smile, staring down at my injury. A dressing covers the stitches on my upper forearm. Thankfully, there was no nerve damage, but it still hurts like hell. "Looks like I'll have to put a bin liner over it and hold it above my head. I won't be long." I rise from the sofa and head upstairs. Though it's only a dozen steps, I'm so tired and exhausted that it feels like I'm scaling Everest.

34

"MARK, I'M NERVOUS," Jane says to me as I pull my van across her drive and we both sit in silence for a few moments staring at her house. Blue and white police tape flutters across her small garden, the only evidence of the attack that took place yesterday.

I look at Jane, who turns to study the rest of her street. A hundred yards back down the road, I spot two neighbours deep in conversation across their shared fence. They glance over in our direction. I'm sure Jane's attack has become the talk, or should I say, gossip of the street.

"You okay?"

Jane nods but remains silent as she chews on her thumbnail.

"You can wait here, and I'll go inside and fetch whatever you need?" I squeeze her hand for reassurance and notice the coldness of her skin. It's fear.

Jane appears lost in her thoughts as she keeps her gaze fixed on a spot beyond my windscreen.

"Jane?"

Shaken from her ruminations, Jane jolts in her seat. "Um, sorry? What did you say?"

With a smile, I squeeze her hand once more. "You don't have to do this if you don't want to. I can go in and get your clothes and whatever else you need."

Jane shakes her head and takes a deep breath. "No. It's my home. I have to, but I'd rather go in there with you than on my own for the first time."

"Well, that's settled. Come on."

I take the lead and stop at her front door before stepping to one side. Jane retrieves her keys from the hoodie I lent her and unlocks the door. She gasps and staggers backwards when she sees the pools of dried blood on her doormat and further trails of blood leading into the lounge. I place an arm around her shoulder. "It's going to be okay. Forensics have completed their investigation. We won't disturb anything." I step around the doormat and take careful steps to avoid the stains on the carpet as I head into the lounge. I glance over my shoulder and see Jane standing there, her mouth wide open, and her eyes wide with fear and shock. It takes a bit of encouragement before she follows in my footsteps and we're both in the lounge.

Jane is fixated on the smears of blood on the wall where she slid down after being attacked by David. I can't imagine what she's thinking or how she's feeling, but her tight grip on my hand gives me an idea.

"I'll need to get someone in to clean this place."

"One thing at a time, Jane. How about you go upstairs and pack the things that you need, and I'll try to tidy up around here for a bit? The quicker we are out of here, the better for you. We can come back in a few days when you feel up to it."

Jane nods as she wraps her hands around her waist

The Ex-Husband

and retraces her steps. I listen as she takes the stairs. With her gone, I stare in disbelief at the carnage and mess around me. There's blood, bandages, dressings, and paper wrappings discarded on the floor, evidence of paramedics tending to Jane and *his* needs. I can't bring myself to mention his name because I feel nothing but rage towards him. If he was here now, I'd beat him black and blue and then drive him to the outskirts of Cambridge and dump him there.

The less Jane sees the better. I step towards the doorway separating the lounge from the hallway and stoop to rip up the bloodstained carpet. The edge comes up easier than expected, and as it pops away from the gripper tracks, I notice black wires buried beneath. Old telephone wires? I doubt it. They're white and stapled to the top edge of skirting boards. I purse my lips. I'm intrigued.

The cables disappear beneath the carpet and under the sofa. I huff and groan as I push and pull the sofa into the middle of the room, careful not to disturb or damage the wiring. The carpet lifts with ease to reveal more black wires that continue along the lounge, past the entrance to the kitchen, and to the furthest corner of the room, where they disappear behind a corner cupboard. I drag the cupboard forward a few inches so I can access the wires which now appear from underneath the carpet and trail up the back of the corner cupboard. It's taller than me, so I grab a chair from the kitchen and stand on it to check the top of the cupboard. I almost miss it.

I take a few seconds to realise what it is as I flick it with my finger. A tiny black camera, half the size of my fingernail. Confusion clouds my thoughts as I step down from the chair and glance around the room. I look down at my feet where I notice the wiring splits off with one thin branch heading into the kitchen. Now it's white to match the kitchen walls and I follow its path to find it's fixed to the architrave around the door frame and there at the very top is another tiny camera, white this time to match its surroundings.

"Jane," I shout from the bottom of the stairs.

"Yeah," she replies as she appears on the landing.

"Silly question, but did you have any miniature cameras installed in your house?"

Jane's look matches my confused face. I scratch my forehead. "I think you need to come down and have a look at this."

Jane joins me in the lounge, and I point out the wiring and discrete cameras.

Her eyes widen in shock and panic. Her mouth opens and closes, but words don't form.

"Has anyone been in your house recently? Like tradesmen?"

Jane shakes her head. She places a hand on her chest. "Oh my God, are those cameras live? Is someone watching me?"

"I don't know, but I've left them and the cabling as it is." A chill races through my body. Though I don't want to say, I think David's being spying on her. I spend the next few minutes tracing the path of the wires as they snake upstairs beneath the stair carpet before trailing off into her bedroom and bathroom. What I discover shocks me further. A small camera positioned above her wardrobe with a view of her bed. Another set of wires leads to her bathroom, where I discover a small camera squeezed between the vents of her extractor fan in the ceiling, and another positioned on top of the wall cabinet. This is worse than I imagined. But where do they lead to? If they

The Ex-Husband 219

are live, they need a feed, and so far I haven't found a transmitter or power source.

Once Jane has gathered all her belongings together, I take her back to the van before I return and head upstairs. I tear through each room searching inside and above cupboards, beneath beds, and anywhere else in case there are further cameras. My search reveals nothing new, but I still can't find the source. I stand with my hands on my hips looking around my surroundings. There's not much of the house that I haven't searched so far. I tip my head back and sigh, and that's when I realise. There's a loft hatch above me.

I race downstairs and retrieve my small ladder and floodlight torch from the back of the van before darting back into the house and upstairs to the landing. I push back the loft hatch and climb into the dark space. It's musty, and dust tickles my nostrils. I flick my torch on. Scattered boxes make access difficult. I rummage around on my hands and knees and it's not long before I discover it. A small transmitter unit connected to a car battery.

I need to call Detective Carter.

David has been watching Jane... and me.

35

I FEEL sick and violated as Mark tells me what he's discovered. My stomach does cartwheels, and bile stings the back of my throat as I hurry to push open the passenger door before I retch and spew over the floor. My head spins and a fine sheen of sweat glistens on my forehead.

"How could he?" I shout, slamming my hand on the dashboard. He's intruded on every aspect of my personal life and my personal dignity. My eyes sting from the tears that spill over.

Mark is also at a loss for words. Only now does he understand the depths to which David will stoop, as he reaches for his phone to call Detective Constable Carter. I wipe the tears away with the back of my hands as I listen to Mark's conversation. He hangs up and sighs.

"Carter is on her way over now. She told us to sit tight and not go back in the house in case we disturb crucial evidence."

"I don't want to go back there. Ever." My hands curl into fists. "Bastard!" I scream.

Mark places a hand on my thigh. His touch is comforting, but it does little to quell the raging ball of anger that burns in my chest. This is typical of David. I remember when our marriage fell apart and the lengths he went to in order to control me. He installed CCTV cameras both inside our house and outside. He wanted to know my every movement when he was at work. There were times I was even too scared to hang out the washing in the back garden in case our neighbours appeared over the fence. I would hang everything on the line as quick as possible before hurrying in. I knew the punishment would be painful if I took too long and stopped to talk to anyone. Even my phone had a tracker on it, so he knew where I was every minute of the day, and he'd come home every night and question my movements.

With a heavy heart, I hang my head in despair. "Mark, I can't believe this."

"I know. But I'm hoping this is good news."

I let out a pathetic laugh. "How can this be good news?" David has watched me walk around my bedroom naked, take a shower, and go to the toilet. He's watched us having sex. He's watched me spending time with Anita.

"Sorry, that wasn't a dig at you." I turn and smile at Mark. "Thank you. I don't think I could cope with all of this without you by my side."

Mark's eyes look beyond me and towards the street before he throws a nod. "Looks like this could be our detective."

I glance behind me to catch sight of a blue Vauxhall Astra approaching our street followed by a white police forensic services van. They pull up close by and I spot Detective Constable Carter step from the Astra accompanied by a male officer. Two other officers exit the white

The Ex-Husband 223

forensic van and retrieve two silver cases from the rear compartment before they join Carter by my front door.

Mark and I step from his van and join them.

"Thank you for coming so quickly." I stuff my hands into the pockets of my hoodie.

Carter nods and turns to Mark. "Is the device in the loft attached to a car battery?"

"Yes. It has a flashing red LED light on it, so it's live and transmitting the feed to somewhere."

Detective Carter turns to the two forensic officers and divides the tasks. One officer is assigned to retrieve the cameras and wiring from the house, while the other is tasked with removing the transmitter and battery from the loft.

We are told to wait outside while Carter and her team head inside. I watch as all the officers snap on nitrile gloves before dispersing in different directions. I can't do anything other than pace around my garden knowing that my house is being scrutinised once again.

"Jane!"

I spin on my heels to see Chrissy march at speed towards me. As I groan and look at Mark, he rolls his eyes. I'm in no mood to talk to her or entertain her need for gossip.

"Jane, my lovely. How are you, darling? I've been so worried about you. We all have. Everyone in the street is talking about you and what happened. I'm so glad you're in one piece. I can't believe I got it so wrong about David. He seemed so nice when he first approached me."

I bet they have been talking.

"How are you?" she asks again. Chrissy places her hand on my good arm.

"I'm okay. It's a lot to take in."

Chrissy looks over my shoulder at my open front door.

"Has something else happened? What are the police doing here again?"

Why don't you go back inside and have your cup of tea and Battenberg slice and mind your own business?

I offer Chrissy a tight smile. "They need to check a few things." I really am in no mood to talk to her. Not because she is nosey, but because I don't want to entertain further thoughts of what happened in there and what David has been privy to. "If you don't mind, I'm not feeling very well, so I'm going to sit in Mark's van. Thank you for your concern. I promise I will catch up with you soon." With that, I walk back to Mark's van, not waiting for a reply.

It's a further twenty minutes before Detective Carter and her team reappear. She instructs us to meet her back at the station to review what they have discovered in an hour. As much as I try to push for answers, she's unwilling to give them to me as she returns to her car.

"I don't know about you, but I could do with a coffee and a bite to eat. Shall we grab something?" Mark suggests, as he starts his van.

"I'm not hungry."

"I know, but it will do you good to get something inside you. Besides, we've got an hour to kill. We can get a drive-through and eat inside the van if you want to?"

To be honest I don't want to eat or drink anything. I feel like I'm trapped in a horrible nightmare. My chest hurts and I can't think. I feel numb. My arm throbs, which reminds me I missed taking my painkillers this morning. But to keep Mark happy I agree as he drives off.

36

"HOW LONG ARE they going to keep us waiting?" I blow out my cheeks and stand. It feels like we've been sitting for ages in the police station waiting for Detective Carter to meet us. In reality it's been only ten or fifteen minutes as I walk over to the noticeboard. It's the same information bulletins I saw on my last visit, including a few pictures of potential suspects that the police are keen to talk to. Each one looks unsavoury, with cold soulless eyes and blank faces. I notice one has a scar running from the corner of his eye down to the side of his mouth and it makes me wonder what caused such a devastating injury.

Mark appears unfazed. He leans forward and rests his elbows on his thighs as he taps his toes. He has more patience than me. I want this over and done with. What happens after all of this is over? Am I still going to be charged with attacking David even though I didn't? How will the police decide who is telling the truth? I know I am but is it enough for them to believe me?

The door clicks open behind me, and I glance round to see Detective Carter appear. She hovers in the doorway and offers me a small smile. "Would you both like to come through?"

Mark stands and joins me by the door, and we follow Detective Carter through a set of fire doors and up a flight of stairs. Uniform and plainclothes officers pass her on the stairs, acknowledging her with a nod. She leads us down another corridor, with smaller offices on either side. As I take a quick peek, I notice a few officers hunched over computer screens, while others sit close to each other in deep discussion.

Detective Carter opens the door and invites us in. "Take a seat."

We do as she says. In front of us is a large table with a laptop and a few folders. Detective Carter sits in front of the laptop and organises her paperwork.

"Sorry to keep you waiting, but we've been analysing the transmitter recovered from your loft. It was piggy-backing off your Wi-Fi and transmitting images from the cameras to a different location. Officers from the high-tech unit have identified a potential IP address."

"IP address?" I lean forward and rest my elbows on the table.

"Yes. It's a unique identifying number assigned to every device connected to the Internet. It offers us a geolocation as well. You have an IP address because you use the Internet and so your IP address is specific to your home address. The data received from the cameras was being sent to a location we believe to be local to Cambridge."

Detective Carter checks we understand before she continues, and we both nod in agreement. "We are still working on a more precise location, but we don't believe the IP address is linked to where David is staying."

I close my eyes and scrunch my face as I try to absorb

the information. "Are you saying it's *not* David? Or you're not sure if it's David?"

"The latter. While David is in hospital and suspected of attacking, we searched his current place of address. He is renting an apartment outside of the city centre. We recovered his laptop and mobile phone from the property, and they are being analysed as we speak."

"It has to be him." I jab my finger on the table.

"So far we have found nothing linked to you or your property. However, we downloaded a copy of his Internet search history, including deleted files and history. Much of his recent history involved search terms related to you."

My eyes widen in shock as I sit back in my chair. "See, I knew it was him."

Detective Carter raises a hand to silence me. "It doesn't tell us anything other than he tried to find out as much as he can about you."

I let out a deep sigh. "Well, he must be staying somewhere else."

"Possibly. Our enquiries are still ongoing. I want to draw your attention to the fact that the transmitter unit also had an internal hard drive for temporary storage." The detective turns to her laptop and after a moment different images appear on the monitor in front of us.

I gasp in horror as my eyes dart between the screen and Mark, who looks shocked as he leans forward. Each screen shows a different part of my house. One shows my lounge, another my kitchen, and the final two screens show my bedroom and bathroom. A burning bitterness stings the back of my mouth, making me feel sick to the pit of my stomach.

"I won't show you all the images to protect your privacy and decency, but you can guess what they contain."

Filled with a mix of embarrassment, shame, and anger, I can't help but bury my head in my hands. This can't be happening. I'm even too embarrassed to look at Mark, as I can only imagine what he's thinking as I hear him clear his throat and shift in his chair.

"Whoever has been spying on you has seen every aspect of your life, and I'm sorry you've experienced this."

My mind darts back to David's escapades with the CCTV in our marital home. "This has to be David. He did something similar when we were married. He wanted to know what I was up to every minute of the day even when he wasn't at home. It was his way of controlling me."

Mark reaches across and rubs the back of my hand. There is a softness in his face as if he can sense the pain I'm experiencing. I'm glad he's here, even though I know it must be difficult for him to see and hear everything being discussed.

"Is there sound to the video feeds?" I turn in my seat towards the detective.

She shakes her head. "Only visual."

"Well, that's something then."

Carter nods in agreement. "There is one last piece of evidence I would like to show you. It's uncomfortable viewing, but important. Are you ready?"

I don't know what she's about to show, and her tone sounds ominous, but I'm already squirming in my seat. "Okay," I reply, reaching out to hold Mark's hand under the table.

The detective clicks on a file and within seconds a video clip plays on the monitor in front of us. It's my confrontation with David. It captures me running from the kitchen through to the lounge where David catches up with me. I watch in silence as the scene unfolds on the screen and for a moment I'm back in my lounge fighting

The Ex-Husband

for my life. I take a sharp intake of breath when he slashes my arm, and I experience the same sting of pain even though I'm sitting in the chair. Though some events feel hazy, and I can't recall them, I'm fixed to the monitor staring in a perverse way to see what happened next.

"Oh my God!" I shout as I'm thrown back in my chair in shock. I watch as David takes a few steps back and stabs himself twice in the leg. I throw my hand over my mouth. He's gone mad. "No!" He wraps my hand around the handle of the knife before collapsing in the front doorway.

Detective Carter pauses the clip. "Your ex-husband staged the entire scene to make it appear as if you attacked him. He transferred your prints to the handle and ran his own bloodied hands down the inside of the door to create the impression he was trying to escape."

My eyes mist over. Seconds later I break down and sob into Mark's chest. He wraps his arms around me and whispers words of comfort.

Detective Carter closes the lid on her laptop. "You have no case to answer. We've been able to prove that David's allegations against you were false and will charge him with GBH and perverting the course of justice."

I pull a tissue from my hoodie and wipe my snotty nose. My eyes feel sore and puffy. "What about the fact that he set up all these cameras and things in my house? And how the hell did he get in?"

"That is something we still need to look into. Until we can confirm the IP address and whether it's linked to David, we cannot tie off that loose end and charge him under the Sexual Offences Act 2003."

"What else can you charge him with?" Mark asks, rubbing my back to soothe my breath which comes in gasps.

"At this moment, nothing other than the GBH and

perverting the course of justice. If we are able to prove that David is behind the camera set up, then we can charge him with observing a private act, recording a private act, and installing equipment to observe a private act. Each one of those is an offence in itself and carries a custodial sentence."

"Thank you, detective." I rub my temples to soothe the pounding in my head. Fatigue and stress leave me broken.

"Jane, you're free to go. I've sent officers to arrest David in the hospital. As soon as he is fit to be moved, I'll interview him under caution here at the station."

The cool air outside bathes my hot face. I should be pleased, but I'm unsure of what to feel. There are so many emotions running through me as I follow Mark back to the van. Anger for what David has done. Sadness for losing my best friend. Guilt for putting Anita in harm's way. From somewhere deep within, I need to find the strength to rebuild my life again.

As I step into the night, a flicker of hope cuts through the chaos. Anger, sadness, guilt—they're all there, but so is something stronger: determination. With Mark by my side, I realise it's time to fight back, to rebuild. This isn't the end. No. This is my chance to start anew, stronger and with eyes wide open.

From here, I take control and grow.

37

FINALLY ALONE, I sit and watch the app on my phone screen. I've not had time to catch up on all the recent recordings, so I'm excited to see what Jane has been up to. Just the chance to see her naked body again and share in her most intimate and private moments sends bolts of nervous excitement coursing through my veins like I've plugged myself into the mains.

I've done a good job of hiding my equipment, and for most people, it could remain hidden and working as long as the transmitter had power.

But as I flick through the most recent recordings, panic grips my chest and dread wipes the smile from my face.

What I didn't plan on or expect was for a qualified sparky to root around Jane's house. He's discovered my equipment and now the police know the truth.

Shit.

38

ONE WEEK LATER...

We both agreed a trip to Portugal was what we needed. And as I sit outside a bar with Mark watching everyday life pass me, and welcome the afternoon sun on my face, there's a sense of freedom that I've not felt for many weeks.

Recent events left me so broken that I wondered if I could ever recover, let alone return to my house. So far I haven't. I don't know what it is, but every time I approach the front door, my heartbeat quickens, my mouth runs dry, and my hands get sweaty. It doesn't matter if I'm on my own or with Mark; the reaction is still the same. There's a psychological block stopping me from taking one step into my house. It's like my behaviour is on loop. I freeze and back away each time Mark opens the door.

Mark has been so supportive. As I hold a glass of wine, he sips from a beer. When I look at him, I realise how grateful I am. I couldn't have got through this without him, and I've told him a million times since.

As I say, every cloud has a silver lining. This is no different. It's been easier to talk with Mark about my past while we've been away. I've kept so much locked away for so long that I wasn't too sure where to start. I guess my story has come out in bits and pieces and Mark has done a fantastic job of patching it all together. He's been sympathetic and understanding. But there's so much more I need to tell him, and I'm ready to let him in on my darkest secrets.

We finish our drinks and walk hand in hand through the backstreets to our hotel. Neither of us talk for most of the journey but enjoy our time together as we stop every so often and peer into the shops along the way.

"Mark, there's something else I need to tell you." I lead him towards the park close by and we take a seat on a bench under a tree, enjoying the dappled shade. A group of young boys play football close by. A huddle of parents sits in a circle on the grass enjoying a picnic, and I spot three old men sitting on a park bench further along the path talking about something as they gesticulate with their arms.

Mark holds my hand as I turn to face him. "This holiday has given me the chance to tell you more about my abusive marriage to David. I never thought I'd be able to tell you half of what I've told you, but after what's happened, the time was right."

"Hey, I understand and I'm not here to judge. I'm so sorry you went through so much trauma and pain. I only wish I'd known you then because I would have taken you away from it much sooner."

His words make me smile, but they make me emotional too as my eyes water. "I know. I wish that too. But at least you know why I have found it hard in the beginning to open up to you physically. There's something

The Ex-Husband 235

important I need to tell you." Mark hangs on my every word and gives me the space I need.

"David raped me many times. And as a result, I fell pregnant once. It's always been my dream to be a mum and to have a family, but David didn't want that. He forced me to have a termination." Tears roll down my cheeks as the memory floods my thoughts. "And, because of how I was abused, and what David did to me, there's a strong risk that I might not be able to have children. I want to be with you more than anything else, but I need you to know that I won't blame you if you want to leave me."

Mark hangs his head and still clutches my hand. I feel sick inside. So much of me wants to get up and run away. The doctors told me I had less than a fifty per cent chance of becoming pregnant again and I've lived with the pain of that news ever since.

We sit in silence for what seems like hours, neither of us knowing what to say. I can see Mark nod as if trying to process the information.

The agony of uncertainty, the shadow of might-not-be's, gnaws at me, a relentless reminder of what was stolen from me. We're ensnared in a moment so dense it's suffocating. I glance at him, his face a mask of contemplation, and desperation claws at my throat. "Say something, Mark."

"Babes, it's a lot to take in, but I'm not going anywhere, I promise. The recent weeks have made me realise how much you mean to me. I've never felt like this before with anyone. Yes, I want a future with you and a family. I've never been happier. Even if there's a chance of you getting pregnant, then we have to hang on to that hope. And if it doesn't work for us, then we can look at adoption. We could give a child such a happy home together."

I smile, and as I'm about to reply, my phone rings. I

pull my phone from my back pocket, and I'm surprised when I see DC Carter's number. "Detective. Is everything okay?"

"Hi, Jane. Sorry to disturb your holiday. Are you enjoying yourself?"

"Yes, thanks. It's very relaxing and Mark and I have had plenty of time to talk and relax after what's happened."

"That's good. I apologise for calling, but I had to reach out as soon as I received the news—there has been a development in your case."

As I purse my lips, I notice Mark mouthing something silently across from me. I put my phone on loudspeaker so he can hear. "Mark and I are both here and the phone is on loudspeaker."

"Oh, that's good. The high-tech team has been working on identifying the IP address at the receiving end of the transmissions. I've got good and bad news."

My heart sinks. A dozen thoughts flash through my mind. Perhaps they haven't been able to tie it back to David. I brace myself for the news.

"I'll give you the bad news first. Unfortunately, the IP address doesn't tie back to David. They've looked at every single angle to be certain. David wasn't spying on you."

The look of shock on Mark's face reflects my own as my jaw falls open. Shit.

"So if it wasn't David, who was it?"

"A colleague of yours. Kiran Bhatt in IT support."

The waves of shock keep hitting me. I sit back on the park bench unable to process what I've heard. I look at Mark and then at my phone. "Kiran?"

"Yes. We traced the IP address back to his house. We executed a warrant and discovered that he had converted

The Ex-Husband

his spare room into a shrine dedicated to you. He had pictures of you taken from a distance. A few photos appear to be from work events that you both attended, a work Christmas party, and a local bar. Other still images from your bedroom turned out to be more revealing and of a sexual nature. He has an infatuation with you. We confiscated his laptop and monitor and that's when we discovered an application on his desktop linked to the cameras secreted in your house."

"Christ." A chill runs down my spine. I've known Kiran for a while now, and he appeared harmless. The computer geek who hid behind his monitor who we'd call when our monitors stopped working, or our computers froze. The person who helped us to recover... files that we've lost. The fact it's not David but someone I say hello to makes his intrusion in my house even more terrifying and humiliating.

"I don't get it. How did he get inside?"

"He's been planning this for a long time and took a lock picking course in his spare time. That's how he entered your house when you were out. And, with his software and hardware skills, he could plant those devices and send live images to his desktop and phone."

Questions rush through my mind. "So the secret admirer's email was from him?"

"No. We suspect that was David. We've not been able to find any evidence of an email being sent from Kiran's laptop or work computer from any of the deleted data we've recovered. David hasn't confessed to it and there's no indication that it was sent from his laptop. But he could have sent it from a library or Internet café."

"Did Kiran admit to stealing my underwear?"

"He did. We also conducted forensic analysis on your

underwear and found a small black hair fibre and semen traces with a DNA profile that matched his. He has also admitted to deleting files from your computer and the main servers. That was deliberate on his part because it meant you would have to contact him, and that's what he wanted." DC Carter pauses for a moment. "Kiran has admitted being infatuated with you for a long time and he was about to admit it to you, but David got in the way."

"Is Kiran being charged?" I ask.

"Yes. We have charged him with criminal trespass for entering your home. We've also charged him with voyeurism under Section 67 of the Sexual Offences Act for observing someone in a private place, recording someone in a private act, and installing cameras with the intention of recording someone in a private act."

I feel my stomach lurch as I think of what Kiran has seen. Bastard.

DC Carter continues. "For a voyeurism charge to be valid and stick, the intent must be of sexual pleasure, and there must be no consent given. As I mentioned, we found his semen stains on the underwear he stole from you, so the intent of self-sexual gratification is there."

I dare not ask but need to. "Is he out?"

"No, Jane. He's been remanded into custody until his trial."

A wave of relief washes over me.

DC Carter updates me on a few other points, including David being held on remand while awaiting his trial. She suggests I pop in to see her upon my return, which I agree to before hanging up.

Mark and I sit in silence staring at each other, both lost for words. All along I thought this was David behind everything. It turns out that Kiran was behind most of it. They both had their own agenda.

The Ex-Husband

"I think it's finally over." I run a hand down my face and let out a long sigh of relief.

Mark wraps his arms around me. We hold each other in silence for ages as life continues around us before we head back to the hotel.

39

It feels odd being back at work, but this time it's a final flying visit as I hand in my resignation letter to Kathy.

"We're sorry to see you go, Jane, but I understand your reasons for wanting to leave," Kathy says from her side of the desk.

We're in her office and not only have I given her my letter, but my ID badge and swipe card for the building. I've spent the last fifteen minutes telling her about David and my marriage, and why my life needs to change.

"I know, and I appreciate it. I thought it would be a hard decision, but my time away has made me see life differently. This place holds great memories and I'll miss everyone so much. But when push comes to shove, I need to stand on my own two feet, and I need to do it somewhere that doesn't carry any ghosts from the past. It's time for a fresh start and new beginnings."

Kathy smiles and nods as her shoulders drop. I sense the emotion building in her as her eyes mist over. She rises from her seat and comes round to my side. I stand,

and she throws her arms around me, which takes me by surprise. I've never seen her like this.

"I'm sorry you had to go through so much. I only wish we could have done more. But thanks to your bravery and experience, I've updated our company policies around workplace harassment and made our tendering process for third-party provider more rigorous so more layers of security are built into our systems and processes."

I feel grateful that Kathy has taken this seriously so that no one else in the business goes through what I've been through. I thank her for her time and head to my floor to say my last goodbyes.

The journey down the stairs feels melancholy as happy memories flood my thoughts. I turn into the corridor and head for the double doors. I freeze as I step through. My breath catches in my throat as I throw a hand to my chest and stare wide-eyed.

My team and work friends huddle together and cheer as I walk in.

"Surprise!" Georgia shouts. "You didn't think you could leave without a proper send off, did you?"

I'm lost for words as I stare at the sea of faces. Brad Ritchie, my director, Georgia, Clive, Annette, Abnash, Priya, and Lucy are there. Even Olu from the post room is there in the crowd along with another few familiar faces.

Georgia rushes to me and grabs me with both hands before hugging me so tight that I can't breathe. "I'm going to miss you so much," she whispers in my ear as the tears well up for both of us.

"Me too," I say as my voice cracks.

"Jesus, woman, you're making my mascara run." Georgia laughs as she steps back.

I smile as Brad pours a glass of Prosecco and hands it to me.

The Ex-Husband

"I'd like to say a few words," Brad shouts. Everyone groans to wind him up, which lightens the mood.

"Just remember you said a *few* words," Clive grouses.

Brad turns to face me. "I know it's shit to see you leave, but I didn't want you to go on a sad note. Jane, you've been an invaluable member of my team, and without you, I would have missed a ton of meetings along with God knows how many tender submission deadlines. I couldn't organise a piss-up in a brewery, but you had this knack of making everything so easy and smooth. So thank you from me and all of us. We'll miss you and keep in touch."

The team cheer and clap in response to Brad's speech. I blush in response, uncomfortable with being the centre of attention, but I pull my shoulders back and embrace it this time. It's the new me.

"Thank you, Brad. And thank you to each one of you for making my time here so special."

The door behind me opens and Kathy slips in. She tiptoes into the group, taking me by surprise. It's a gesture I never expected from my HR manager.

I continue. "I want to say a special thanks to my bestie, Georgia. She has always been here for me, and I would be lost without her... and more sober!"

The team erupts into a crescendo of laugher. Georgia pulls a face and points at me before blowing me a kiss.

Over the next forty minutes we talk and laugh as a team, and I make sure I go round to each person thanking them and saying my goodbyes.

Georgia walks me to the front door where Mark is waiting in his van. We step outside and face each other, neither one knowing what to say because it will feel so final. After a few moments, I reach across and pull her in for an embrace. I'm filled with a glowing warmth and a swell of sadness, and I don't know how to handle it.

"I'm so going to miss you, Georgia. Thank you for being my rock here."

The tears roll down Georgia's face and she's too choked up to reply. I wipe away her tears with my thumbs and kiss her on the cheek as I walk away and step into Mark's van. With a last wave and blow of a kiss, Mark pulls away and I'm left staring at Georgia as she disappears into the distance.

40

IT'S BEEN a few days since DC Carter's call, and it feels odd coming down my road. Mark is with me at his insistence. He didn't want me returning home alone to gather more of my belongings. We've already decided that I'm going to sell up and buy a house in a small village on the outskirts of Bury St Edmunds and Mark's going to come with me. I need a fresh start with a new job, new house, and new neighbours. The problem with staying in Cambridge is that there are too many painful memories there now. Most of the city streets remind me of my encounters with David. My house reminds me of where he attacked me and where Kiran invaded my privacy.

There is still a sense of sadness that follows me. The officers investigating Anita's death haven't been able to find anything linking David to the scene. They know someone broke in through the back, but they've not been able to link anything forensically to David, and that hurts. I still know in my heart that David was responsible, and it pains me to think he'll get away with her murder.

Mark pulls up on to my drive and I step out as he

retrieves a few empty boxes and a case from the back of his van. As I wait for him, I notice a bouquet resting against my doorstep.

Mark stands to one side to allow me to pass, and I reach down to pick up the bouquet. It's a rich and vibrant spray of flowers that smells delightful. I imagine they are from work or from my neighbours welcoming me home. I pull the note out. It's blank on one side and as I flip it over, I freeze and my blood runs cold. My hand trembles. There's a message which says,

I'll never let you go. D xx

"Oh my God, Mark. He won't leave me alone."

Mark lets go of the boxes and case and rushes to embrace me as my legs go weak and my body goes limp. The flowers flutter to the ground. "I've got you. I won't let that bastard get anywhere near you. We need to call DC Carter."

The sight of those flowers, and a twisted message from David, sends a jolt of pain through me, but I refuse to crumble. I feel broken inside and it's like someone has peeled the scab away from a newly healed wound as the pain hits me again and my chest tightens. I can't let this happen again. Never again. I push back from Mark and stamp down on the bouquet. My heart may ache, but it beats stronger with defiance. My voice breaks the silence. A roar of liberation against the chains he tries to impose from behind bars.

"No, you will not win! You can't control me!" I scream as I let out all my pent-up anger and frustration on the bouquet. I crush the petals beneath my feet, each stomp a declaration of my resilience. I've been through hell and back, and refuse to be intimidated by David's pathetic and lingering attempt at control. With him on remand in

The Ex-Husband 247

prison, I tell myself that he can't hurt me and once I have moved, he'll never find me again.

I'm a survivor.

A fighter.

With David locked away, his reach is limited to these pathetic gestures. And as I plan my escape, to vanish beyond his grasp, I know with fierce certainty: I am also strong beyond measure.

He will never, ever break me.

Subscribe to my newsletter and receive your FREE ebook of *The Unwelcome Guest* that's only available to my VIP reader group:

aaronquinnbooks.com

CURRENT BOOK LIST

Hop over to my website for a current list of books:
https://aaronquinnbooks.com/books/

OTHER WAYS TO STAY IN TOUCH

Other ways you can connect with me:

Facebook: Aaron-Quinn Author

TikTok: Aaron Quinn Author

Email aaron@aaronquinnbooks.com with any questions, ideas or interesting story suggestions. Hey, even if you spot a typo that we've missed, then drop me a line!

ABOUT THE AUTHOR

I live in Essex in the UK and love spending time people watching and wandering the fields and forests of my county.

Before my writing career, I worked in HR within the Financial Services Sector, and then retrained as Mind Coach, before becoming a full-time author in 2015. I've always been fascinated by people, how the mind works, and the raw emotions that drive us to do the things we do.

I write dark, gripping, domestic thrillers about ordinary people in extraordinary situations. In fact, the very same people who live next door to you, or you say hi to every day. Have you ever wondered what goes on behind closed doors? Well perhaps I can enlighten you through my books.

When I'm not writing, at the gym, or playing with the 4 Yorkies in our family, you'll find me people-watching and imagining what kind of life they *really* lead.

Printed in Great Britain
by Amazon